DISNEP

THE
LION KING

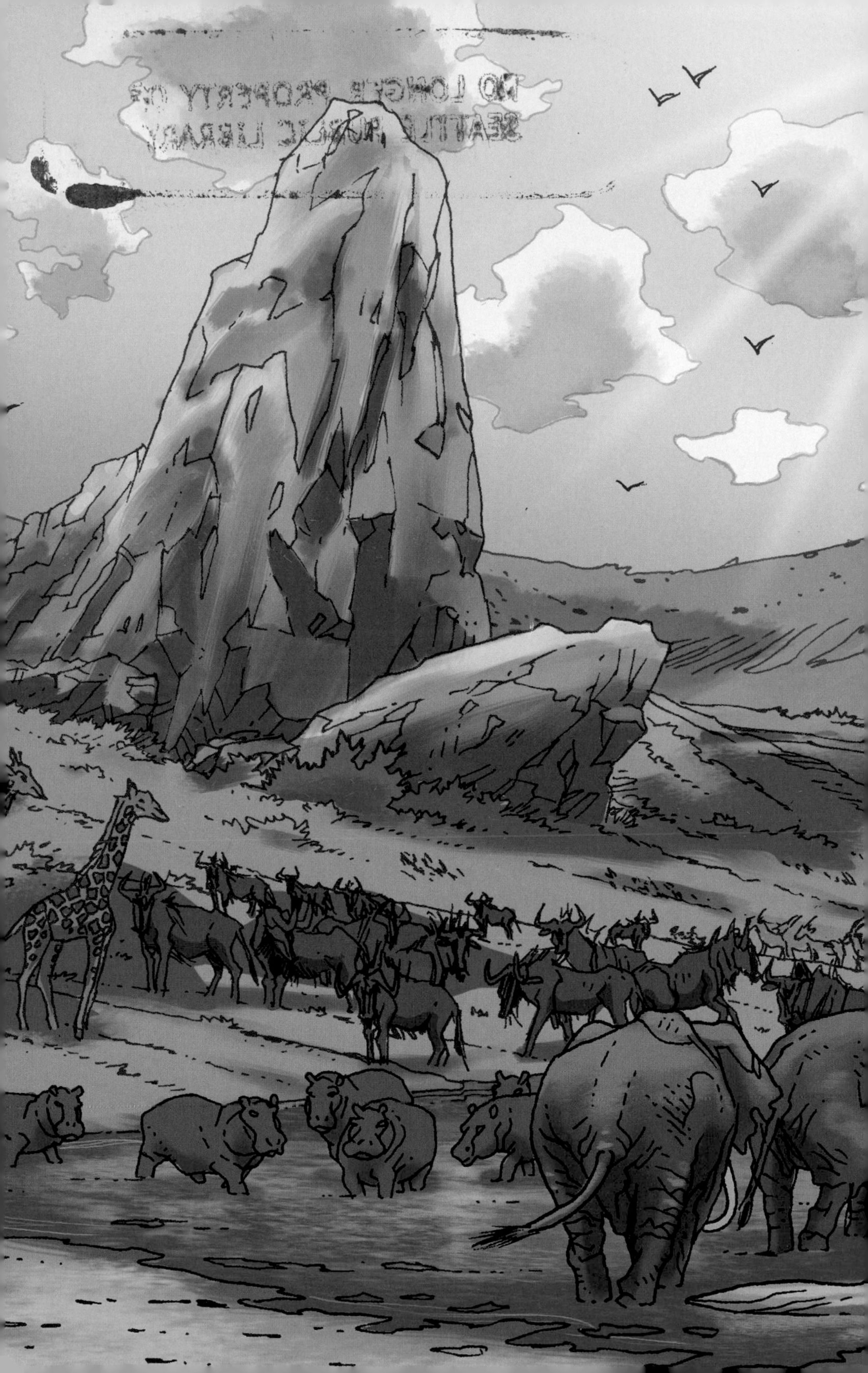

DISNEY

THE LION KING

WILD SCHEMES AND CATASTROPHES

Script
JOHN JACKSON MILLER

Art
TIMOTHY GREEN II
DANILO ANTONIUCCI
ALEXANDRA FASTOVETS

Colors
JORDI ESCUIN LLORACH
DANILO ANTONIUCCI
JULIA ZHURAVLEVA

Lettering
RICHARD STARKINGS and
COMICRAFT'S JIMMY BETANCOURT

Cover Art
TIMOTHY GREEN II with
JORDI ESCUIN LLORACH

Dark Horse Books

Dark Horse Books

President and Publisher **Mike Richardson**

Editor **Freddye Miller**

Assistant Editor **Judy Khuu**

Designer **Anita Magaña**

Digital Art Technician **Christianne Gillenardo-Goudreau**

Neil Hankerson, Executive Vice President • **Tom Weddle**, Chief Financial Officer • **Randy Stradley**, Vice President of Publishing • **Nick McWhorter**, Chief Business Development Officer • **Dale LaFountain**, Chief Information Officer • **Matt Parkinson**, Vice President of Marketing • **Cara Niece**, Vice President of Production and Scheduling • **Mark Bernardi**, Vice President of Book Trade and Digital Sales • **Ken Lizzi**, General Counsel • **Dave Marshall**, Editor in Chief • **Davey Estrada**, Editorial Director • **Chris Warner**, Senior Books Editor • **Cary Grazzini**, Director of Specialty Projects • **Lia Ribacchi**, Art Director • **Vanessa Todd-Holmes**, Director of Print Purchasing • **Matt Dryer**, Director of Digital Art and Prepress • **Michael Gombos**, Senior Director of Licensed Publications • **Kari Yadro**, Director of Custom Programs • **Kari Torson**, Director of International Licensing • **Sean Brice**, Director of Trade Sales

Disney Publishing Worldwide Global Magazines, Comics And Partworks

Publisher Lynn Waggoner • **Editorial Team** Bianca Coletti (Director, Magazines), Guido Frazzini (Director, Comics), Carlotta Quattrocolo (Executive Editor), Stefano Ambrosio (Executive Editor, New IP), Camilla Vedove (Senior Manager, Editorial Development), Behnoosh Khalili (Senior Editor), Julie Dorris (Senior Editor), Mina Riazi (Assistant Editor), Jonathan Manning (Assistant Editor) • **Design** Enrico Soave (Senior Designer) • **Art** Ken Shue (VP, Global Art), Manny Mederos (Senior Illustration Manager, Comics and Magazines), Roberto Santillo (Creative Director), Marco Ghiglione (Creative Manager), Stefano Attardi (Computer Art Designer) • **Portfolio Management** Olivia Ciancarelli (Director) • **Business & Marketing** Mariantonietta Galla (Marketing Manager), Virpi Korhonen (Editorial Manager)

"King for a Day" & "Snow Day" art by **Timothy Green II** with colors by **Jordi Escuin Llorach**
"Keeper of the Egg" art and colors by **Danilo Antoniucci**
"Bad Omens" art by **Alexandra Fastovets** with colors by **Julia Zhuravleva**

Disney The Lion King: Wild Schemes and Catastrophes
Copyright © 2019 Disney Enterprises, Inc. All Rights Reserved. Dark Horse Books® and the Dark Horse logo are registered trademarks of Dark Horse Comics LLC. All rights reserved. No portion of this publication may be reproduced or transmitted, in any form or by any means, without the express written permission of Dark Horse Comics LLC. Names, characters, places, and incidents featured in this publication either are the product of the author's imagination or are used fictitiously. Any resemblance to actual persons (living or dead), events, institutions, or locales, without satiric intent, is coincidental.

Published by Dark Horse Books
A division of Dark Horse Comics LLC
10956 SE Main Street
Milwaukie, OR 97222

DarkHorse.com
To find a comics shop in your area, visit comicshoplocator.com

First edition: June 2019
ISBN 978-1-50671-273-4
Digital ISBN 978-1-50671-292-5
10 9 8 7 6 5 4 3 2 1
Printed in the United States of America

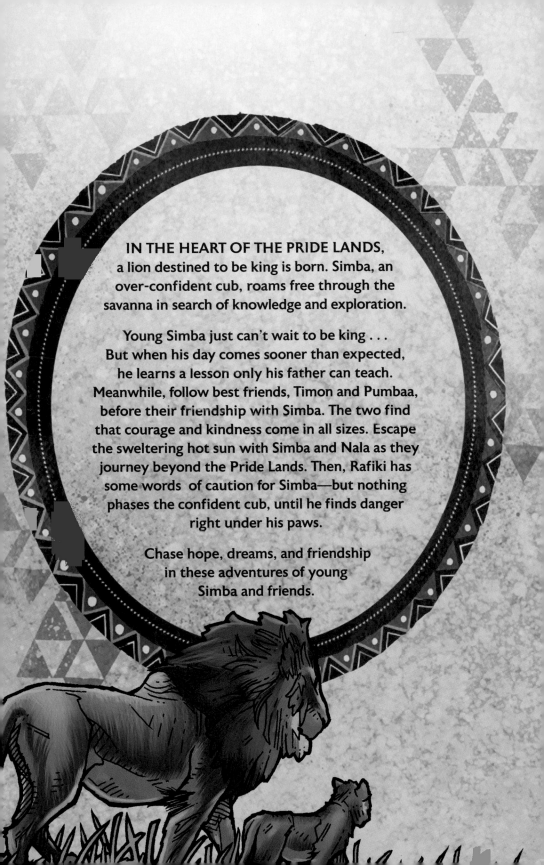

IN THE HEART OF THE PRIDE LANDS,
a lion destined to be king is born. Simba, an
over-confident cub, roams free through the
savanna in search of knowledge and exploration.

Young Simba just can't wait to be king . . .
But when his day comes sooner than expected,
he learns a lesson only his father can teach.
Meanwhile, follow best friends, Timon and Pumbaa,
before their friendship with Simba. The two find
that courage and kindness come in all sizes. Escape
the sweltering hot sun with Simba and Nala as they
journey beyond the Pride Lands. Then, Rafiki has
some words of caution for Simba—but nothing
phases the confident cub, until he finds danger
right under his paws.

Chase hope, dreams, and friendship
in these adventures of young
Simba and friends.

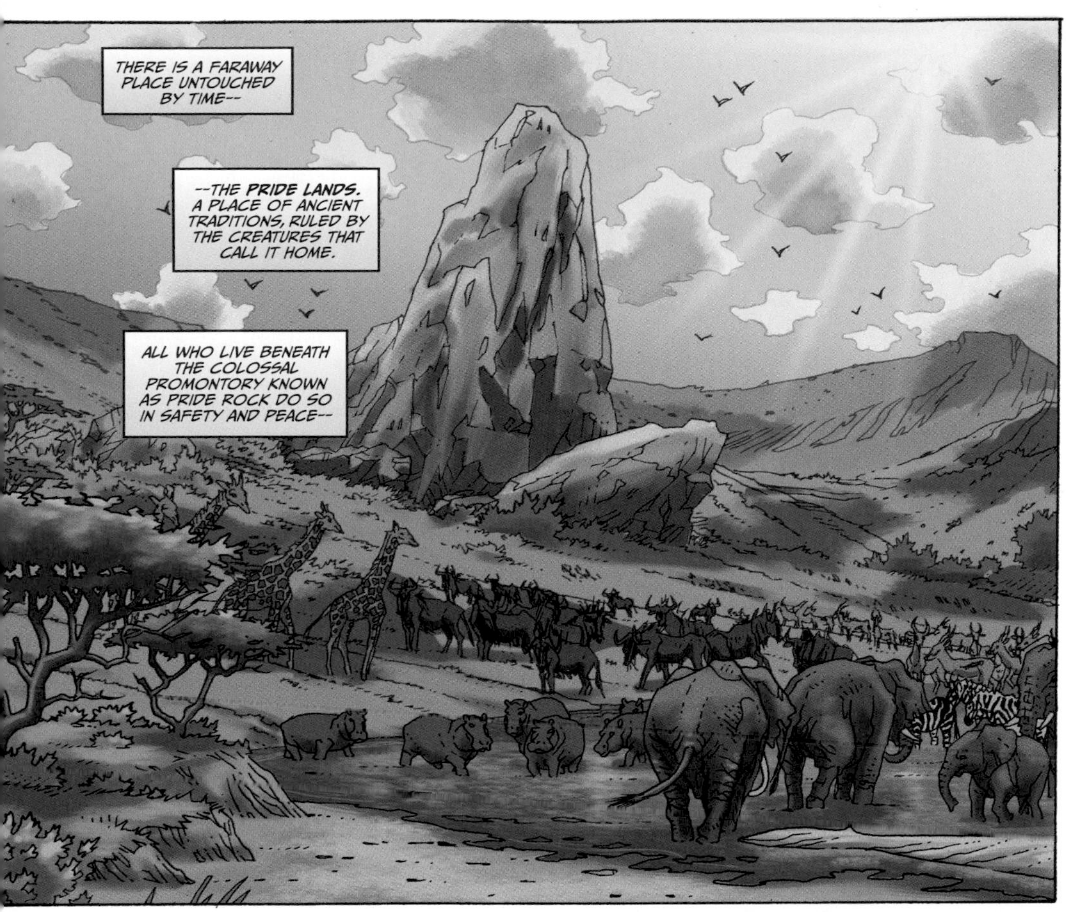
THERE IS A FARAWAY PLACE UNTOUCHED BY TIME--
--THE PRIDE LANDS. A PLACE OF ANCIENT TRADITIONS, RULED BY THE CREATURES THAT CALL IT HOME.
ALL WHO LIVE BENEATH THE COLOSSAL PROMONTORY KNOWN AS PRIDE ROCK DO SO IN SAFETY AND PEACE--

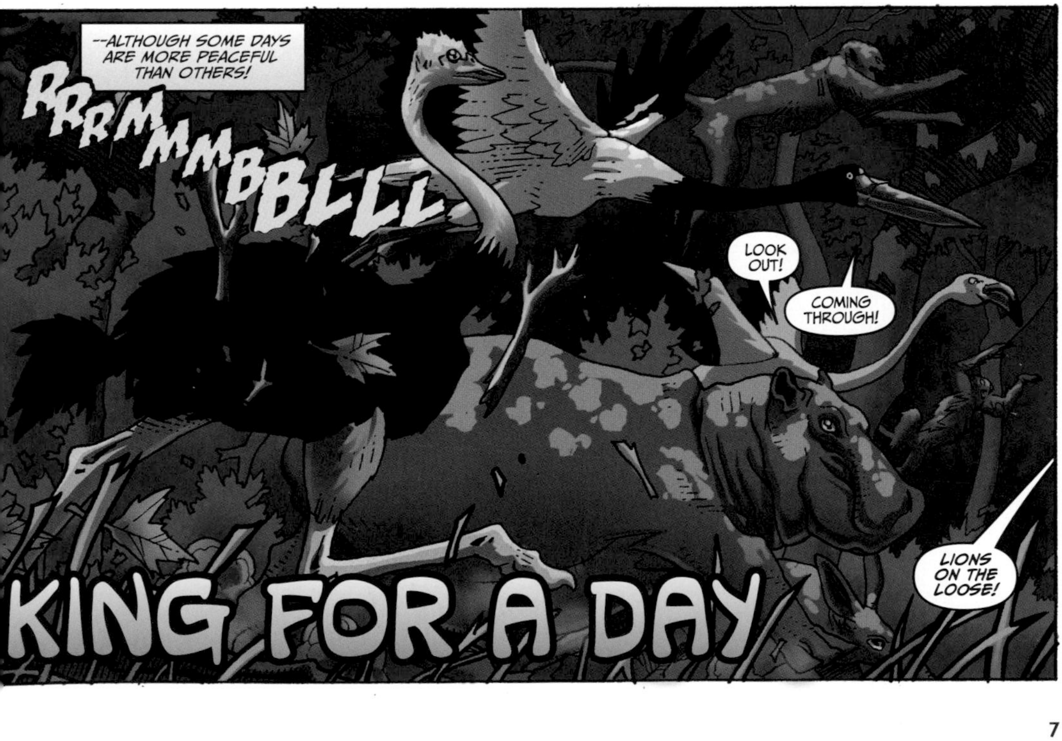
--ALTHOUGH SOME DAYS ARE MORE PEACEFUL THAN OTHERS!
RRRMMMBBLLL
LOOK OUT!
COMING THROUGH!
LIONS ON THE LOOSE!
KING FOR A DAY

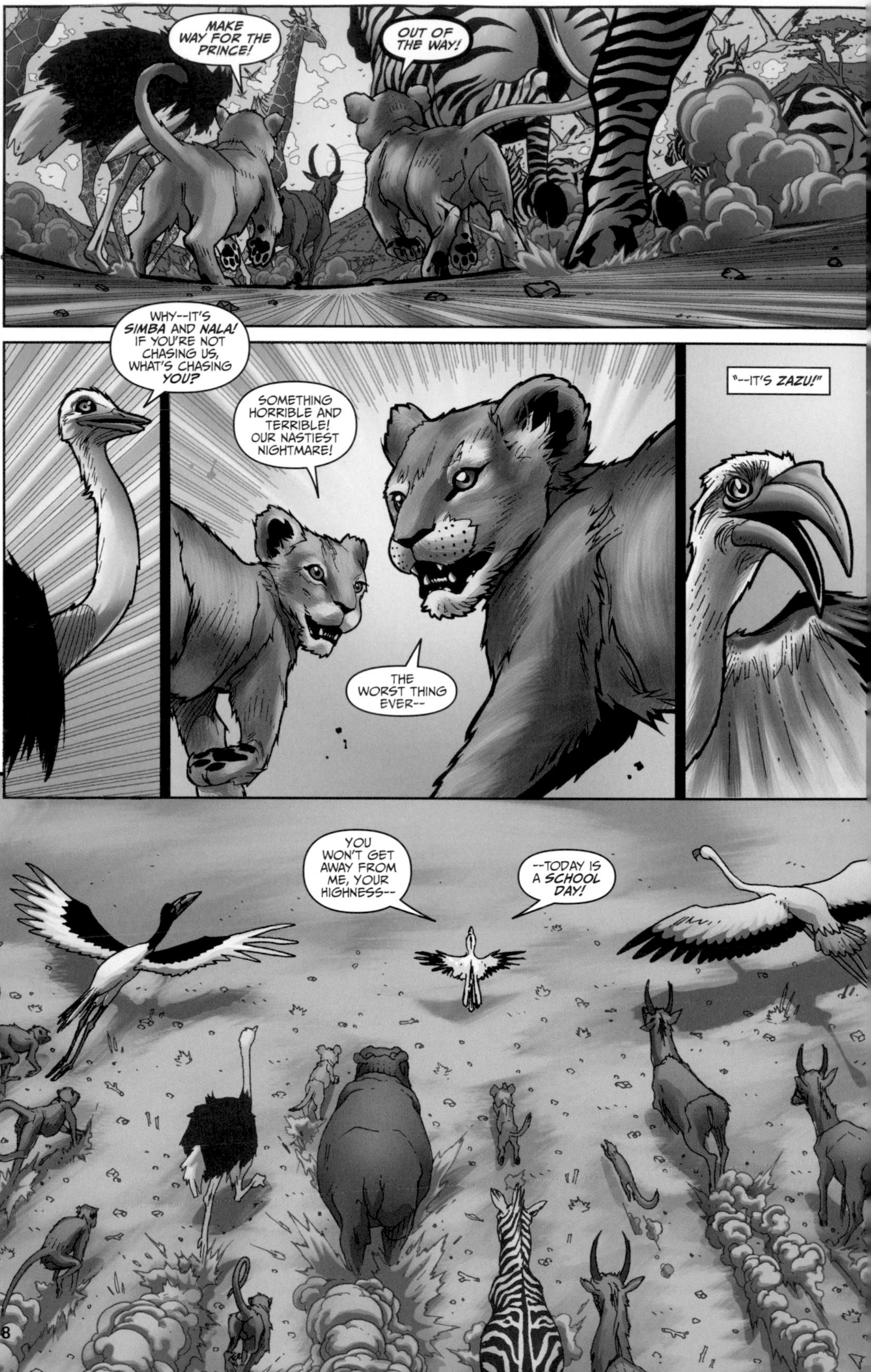
MAKE WAY FOR THE PRINCE!
OUT OF THE WAY!
WHY--IT'S SIMBA AND NALA! IF YOU'RE NOT CHASING US, WHAT'S CHASING YOU?
SOMETHING HORRIBLE AND TERRIBLE! OUR NASTIEST NIGHTMARE!
THE WORST THING EVER--
"--IT'S ZAZU!"
YOU WON'T GET AWAY FROM ME, YOUR HIGHNESS--
--TODAY IS A SCHOOL DAY!

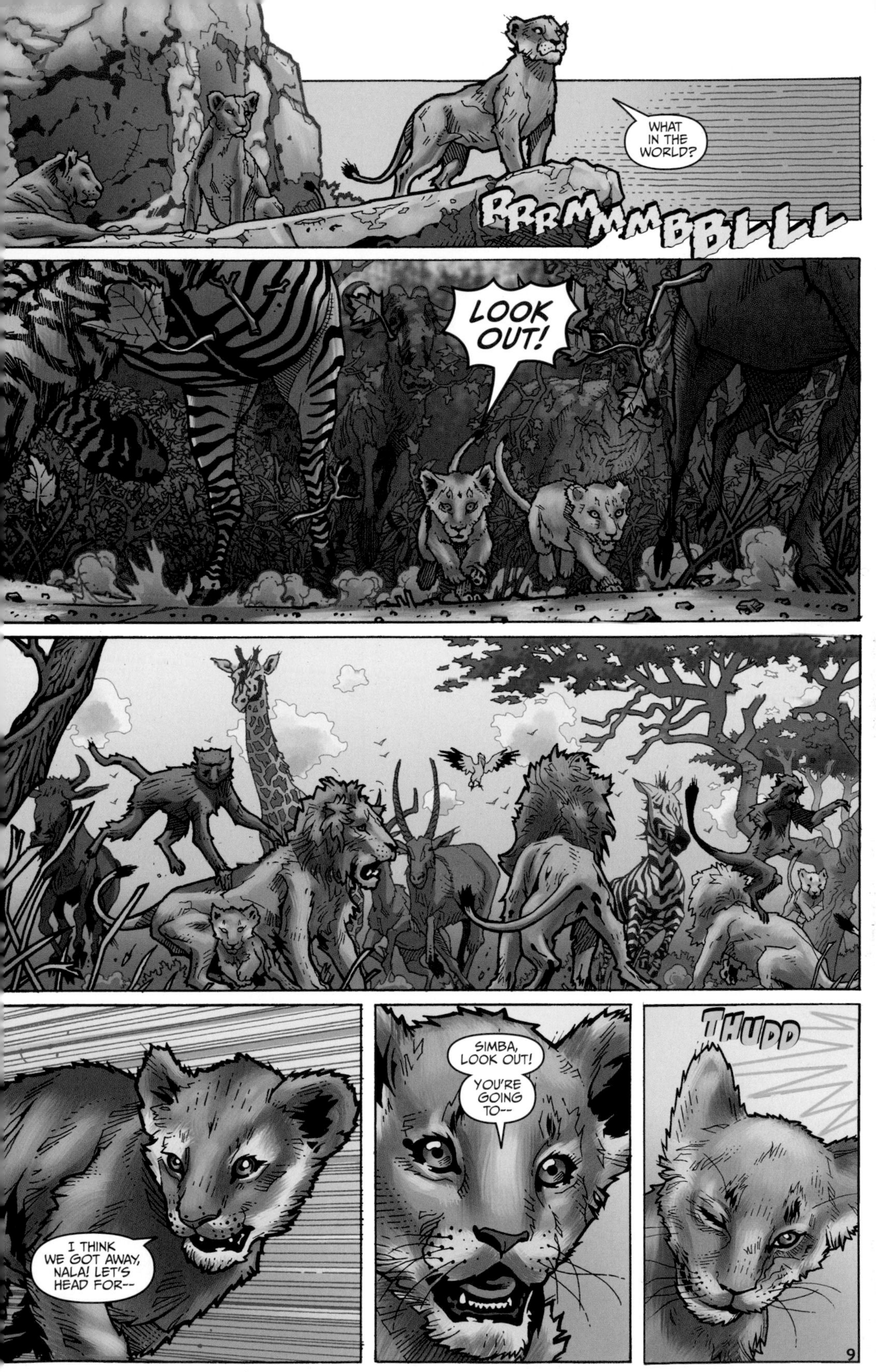
WHAT IN THE WORLD?
RRRMMMBBLLL
LOOK OUT!
I THINK WE GOT AWAY, NALA! LET'S HEAD FOR--
SIMBA, LOOK OUT!
YOU'RE GOING TO--
THUDD

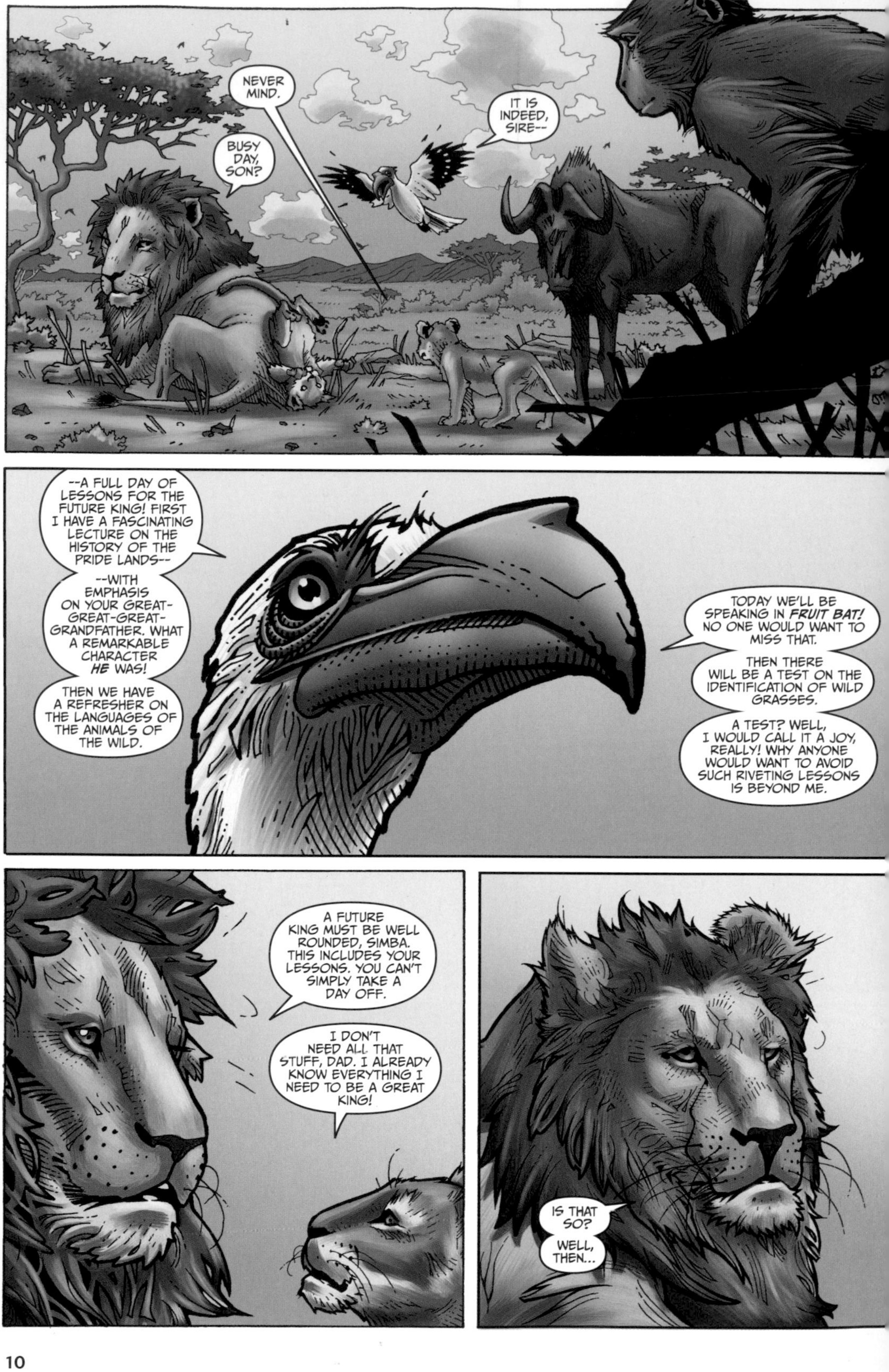
NEVER MIND.
BUSY DAY, SON?
IT IS INDEED, SIRE--
--A FULL DAY OF LESSONS FOR THE FUTURE KING! FIRST I HAVE A FASCINATING LECTURE ON THE HISTORY OF THE PRIDE LANDS--
--WITH EMPHASIS ON YOUR GREAT-GREAT-GREAT-GRANDFATHER. WHAT A REMARKABLE CHARACTER HE WAS!
THEN WE HAVE A REFRESHER ON THE LANGUAGES OF THE ANIMALS OF THE WILD.
TODAY WE'LL BE SPEAKING IN FRUIT BAT! NO ONE WOULD WANT TO MISS THAT.
THEN THERE WILL BE A TEST ON THE IDENTIFICATION OF WILD GRASSES.
A TEST? WELL, I WOULD CALL IT A JOY, REALLY! WHY ANYONE WOULD WANT TO AVOID SUCH RIVETING LESSONS IS BEYOND ME.
A FUTURE KING MUST BE WELL ROUNDED, SIMBA. THIS INCLUDES YOUR LESSONS. YOU CAN'T SIMPLY TAKE A DAY OFF.
I DON'T NEED ALL THAT STUFF, DAD. I ALREADY KNOW EVERYTHING I NEED TO BE A GREAT KING!
IS THAT SO?
WELL, THEN...

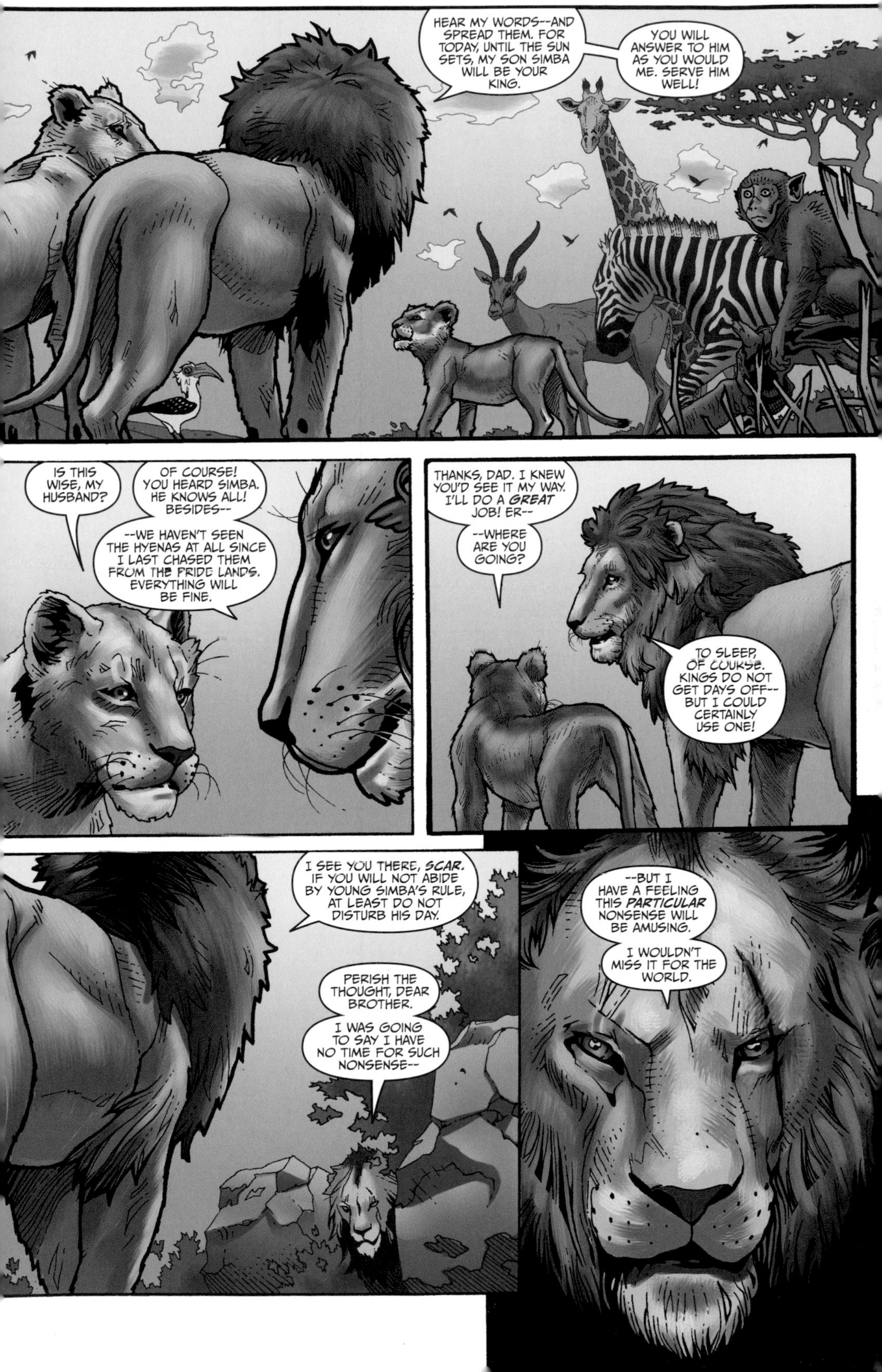
HEAR MY WORDS--AND SPREAD THEM. FOR TODAY, UNTIL THE SUN SETS, MY SON SIMBA WILL BE YOUR KING.
YOU WILL ANSWER TO HIM AS YOU WOULD ME. SERVE HIM WELL!
IS THIS WISE, MY HUSBAND?
OF COURSE! YOU HEARD SIMBA. HE KNOWS ALL! BESIDES--
--WE HAVEN'T SEEN THE HYENAS AT ALL SINCE I LAST CHASED THEM FROM THE PRIDE LANDS. EVERYTHING WILL BE FINE.
THANKS, DAD. I KNEW YOU'D SEE IT MY WAY. I'LL DO A GREAT JOB! ER--
--WHERE ARE YOU GOING?
TO SLEEP, OF COURSE. KINGS DO NOT GET DAYS OFF--BUT I COULD CERTAINLY USE ONE!
I SEE YOU THERE, SCAR. IF YOU WILL NOT ABIDE BY YOUNG SIMBA'S RULE, AT LEAST DO NOT DISTURB HIS DAY.
PERISH THE THOUGHT, DEAR BROTHER.
I WAS GOING TO SAY I HAVE NO TIME FOR SUCH NONSENSE--
--BUT I HAVE A FEELING THIS PARTICULAR NONSENSE WILL BE AMUSING.
I WOULDN'T MISS IT FOR THE WORLD.

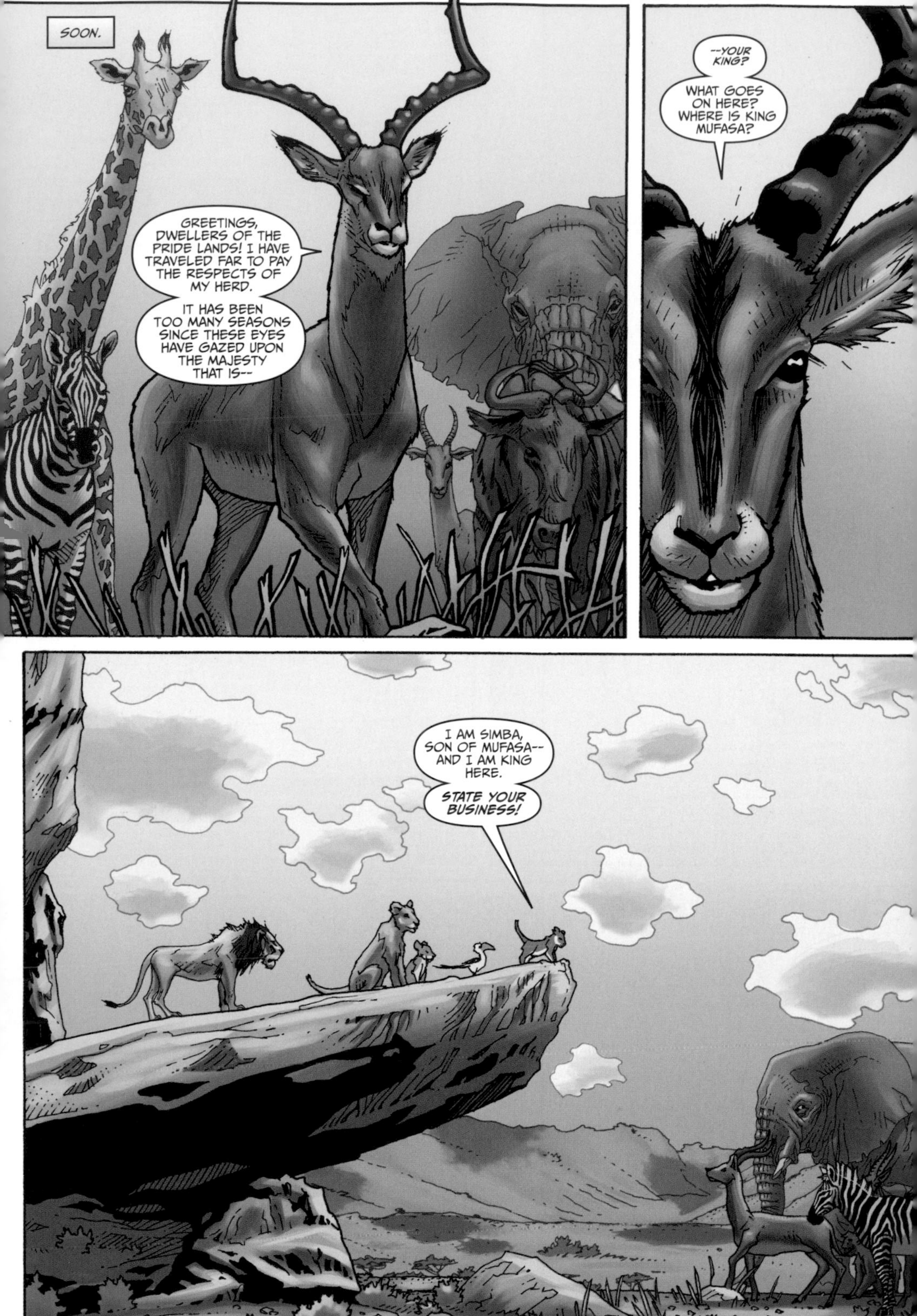
SOON.
GREETINGS, DWELLERS OF THE PRIDE LANDS! I HAVE TRAVELED FAR TO PAY THE RESPECTS OF MY HERD.
IT HAS BEEN TOO MANY SEASONS SINCE THESE EYES HAVE GAZED UPON THE MAJESTY THAT IS--
--YOUR KING?
WHAT GOES ON HERE? WHERE IS KING MUFASA?
I AM SIMBA, SON OF MUFASA-- AND I AM KING HERE.
STATE YOUR BUSINESS!

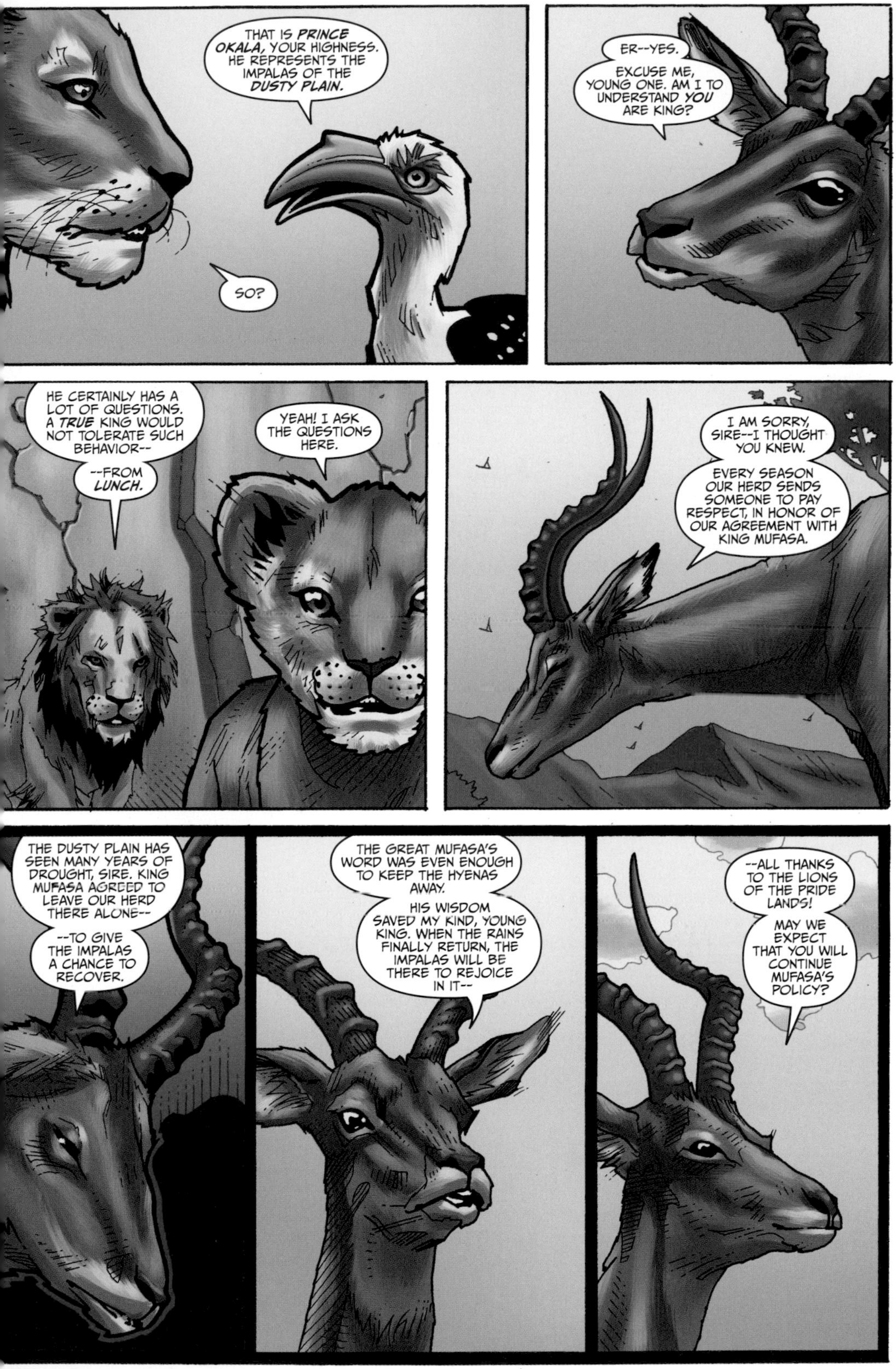
THAT IS PRINCE OKALA, YOUR HIGHNESS. HE REPRESENTS THE IMPALAS OF THE DUSTY PLAIN.
SO?
ER--YES.
EXCUSE ME, YOUNG ONE. AM I TO UNDERSTAND YOU ARE KING?
HE CERTAINLY HAS A LOT OF QUESTIONS. A TRUE KING WOULD NOT TOLERATE SUCH BEHAVIOR--
--FROM LUNCH.
YEAH! I ASK THE QUESTIONS HERE.
I AM SORRY, SIRE--I THOUGHT YOU KNEW.
EVERY SEASON OUR HERD SENDS SOMEONE TO PAY RESPECT, IN HONOR OF OUR AGREEMENT WITH KING MUFASA.
THE DUSTY PLAIN HAS SEEN MANY YEARS OF DROUGHT, SIRE. KING MUFASA AGREED TO LEAVE OUR HERD THERE ALONE--
--TO GIVE THE IMPALAS A CHANCE TO RECOVER.
THE GREAT MUFASA'S WORD WAS EVEN ENOUGH TO KEEP THE HYENAS AWAY.
HIS WISDOM SAVED MY KIND, YOUNG KING. WHEN THE RAINS FINALLY RETURN, THE IMPALAS WILL BE THERE TO REJOICE IN IT--
--ALL THANKS TO THE LIONS OF THE PRIDE LANDS!
MAY WE EXPECT THAT YOU WILL CONTINUE MUFASA'S POLICY?

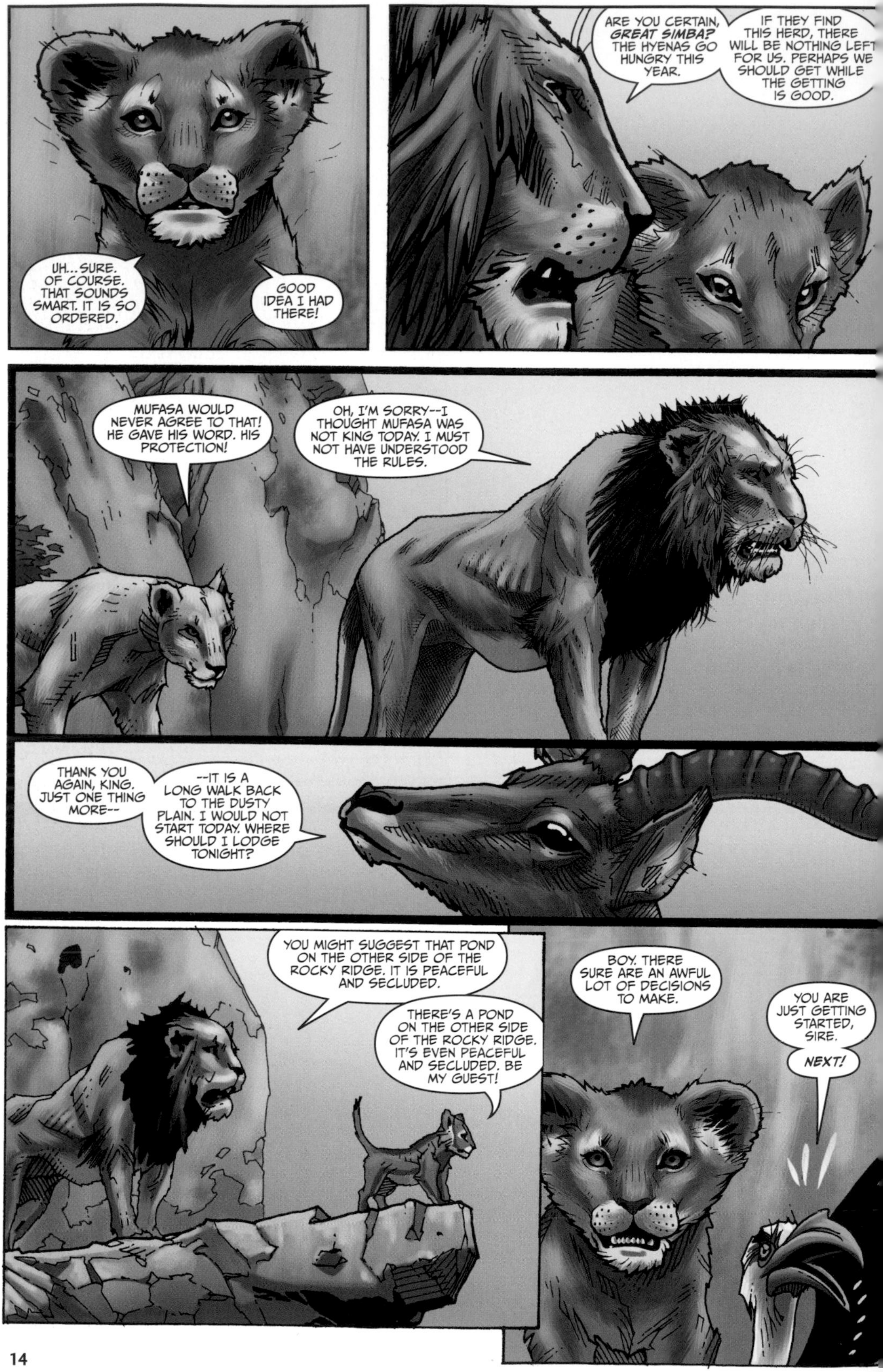

UH... SURE. OF COURSE. THAT SOUNDS SMART. IT IS SO ORDERED.
GOOD IDEA I HAD THERE!
ARE YOU CERTAIN, GREAT SIMBA? THE HYENAS GO HUNGRY THIS YEAR.
IF THEY FIND THIS HERD, THERE WILL BE NOTHING LEFT FOR US. PERHAPS WE SHOULD GET WHILE THE GETTING IS GOOD.
MUFASA WOULD NEVER AGREE TO THAT! HE GAVE HIS WORD. HIS PROTECTION!
OH, I'M SORRY--I THOUGHT MUFASA WAS NOT KING TODAY. I MUST NOT HAVE UNDERSTOOD THE RULES.
THANK YOU AGAIN, KING. JUST ONE THING MORE--
--IT IS A LONG WALK BACK TO THE DUSTY PLAIN. I WOULD NOT START TODAY. WHERE SHOULD I LODGE TONIGHT?
YOU MIGHT SUGGEST THAT POND ON THE OTHER SIDE OF THE ROCKY RIDGE. IT IS PEACEFUL AND SECLUDED.
THERE'S A POND ON THE OTHER SIDE OF THE ROCKY RIDGE. IT'S EVEN PEACEFUL AND SECLUDED. BE MY GUEST!
BOY. THERE SURE ARE AN AWFUL LOT OF DECISIONS TO MAKE.
YOU ARE JUST GETTING STARTED, SIRE.
NEXT!

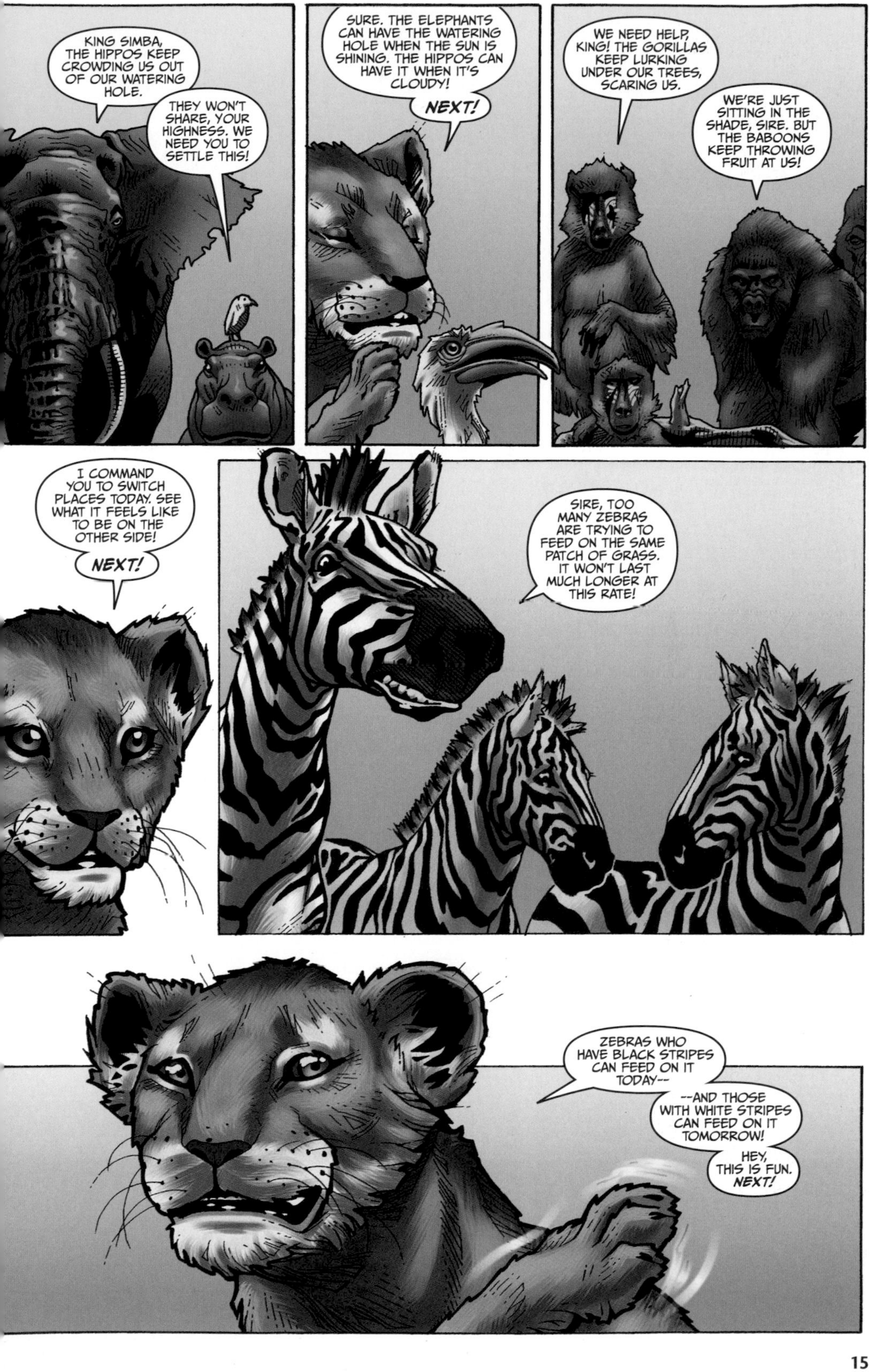

KING SIMBA, THE HIPPOS KEEP CROWDING US OUT OF OUR WATERING HOLE.
THEY WON'T SHARE, YOUR HIGHNESS. WE NEED YOU TO SETTLE THIS!
SURE. THE ELEPHANTS CAN HAVE THE WATERING HOLE WHEN THE SUN IS SHINING. THE HIPPOS CAN HAVE IT WHEN IT'S CLOUDY!
NEXT!
WE NEED HELP, KING! THE GORILLAS KEEP LURKING UNDER OUR TREES, SCARING US.
WE'RE JUST SITTING IN THE SHADE, SIRE. BUT THE BABOONS KEEP THROWING FRUIT AT US!
I COMMAND YOU TO SWITCH PLACES TODAY. SEE WHAT IT FEELS LIKE TO BE ON THE OTHER SIDE!
NEXT!
SIRE, TOO MANY ZEBRAS ARE TRYING TO FEED ON THE SAME PATCH OF GRASS. IT WON'T LAST MUCH LONGER AT THIS RATE!
ZEBRAS WHO HAVE BLACK STRIPES CAN FEED ON IT TODAY--
--AND THOSE WITH WHITE STRIPES CAN FEED ON IT TOMORROW!
HEY, THIS IS FUN. NEXT!

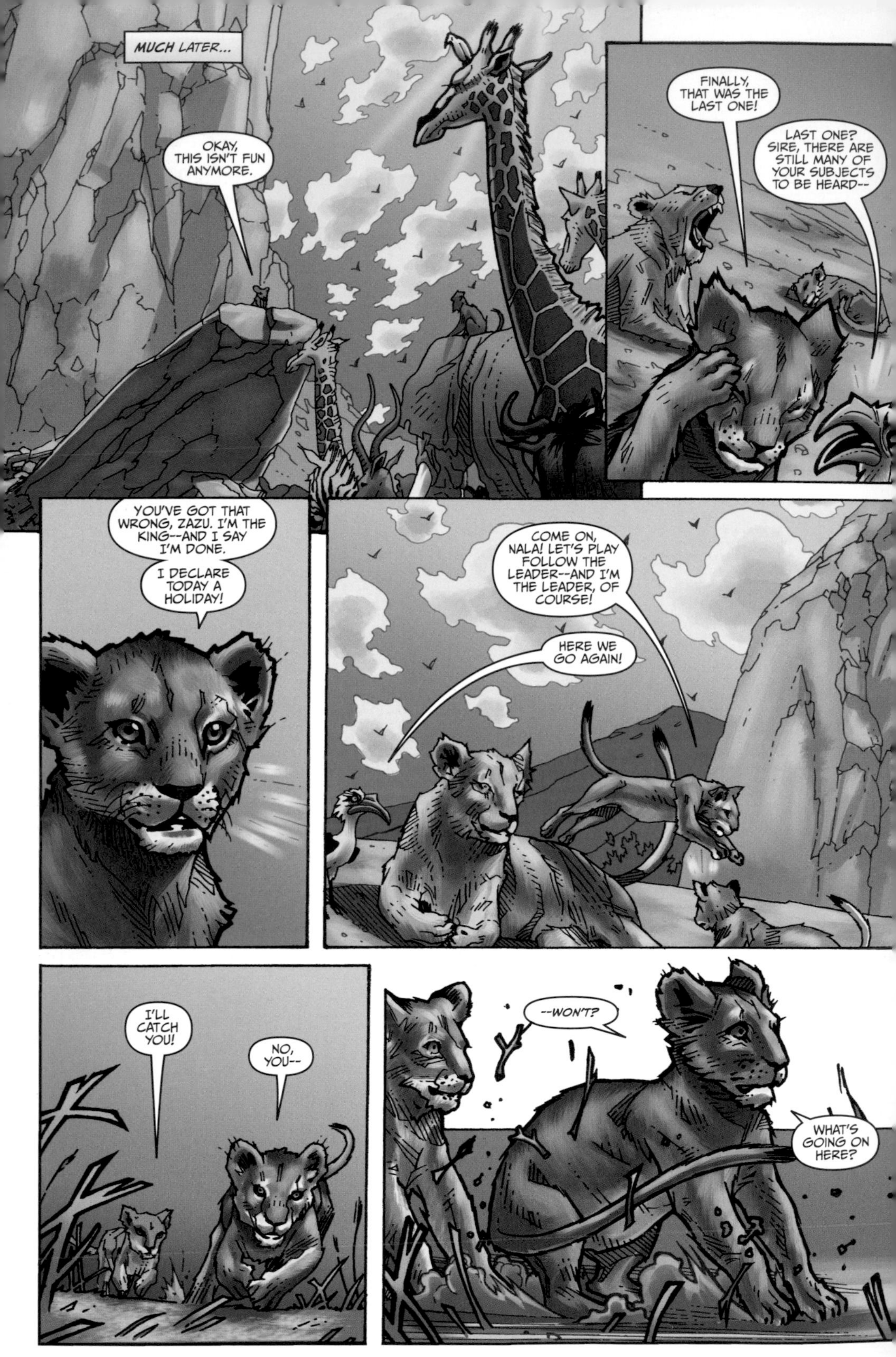
MUCH LATER...
OKAY, THIS ISN'T FUN ANYMORE.
FINALLY, THAT WAS THE LAST ONE!
LAST ONE? SIRE, THERE ARE STILL MANY OF YOUR SUBJECTS TO BE HEARD--
YOU'VE GOT THAT WRONG, ZAZU. I'M THE KING--AND I SAY I'M DONE.
I DECLARE TODAY A HOLIDAY!
COME ON, NALA! LET'S PLAY FOLLOW THE LEADER--AND I'M THE LEADER, OF COURSE!
HERE WE GO AGAIN!
I'LL CATCH YOU!
NO, YOU--
--WON'T?
WHAT'S GOING ON HERE?

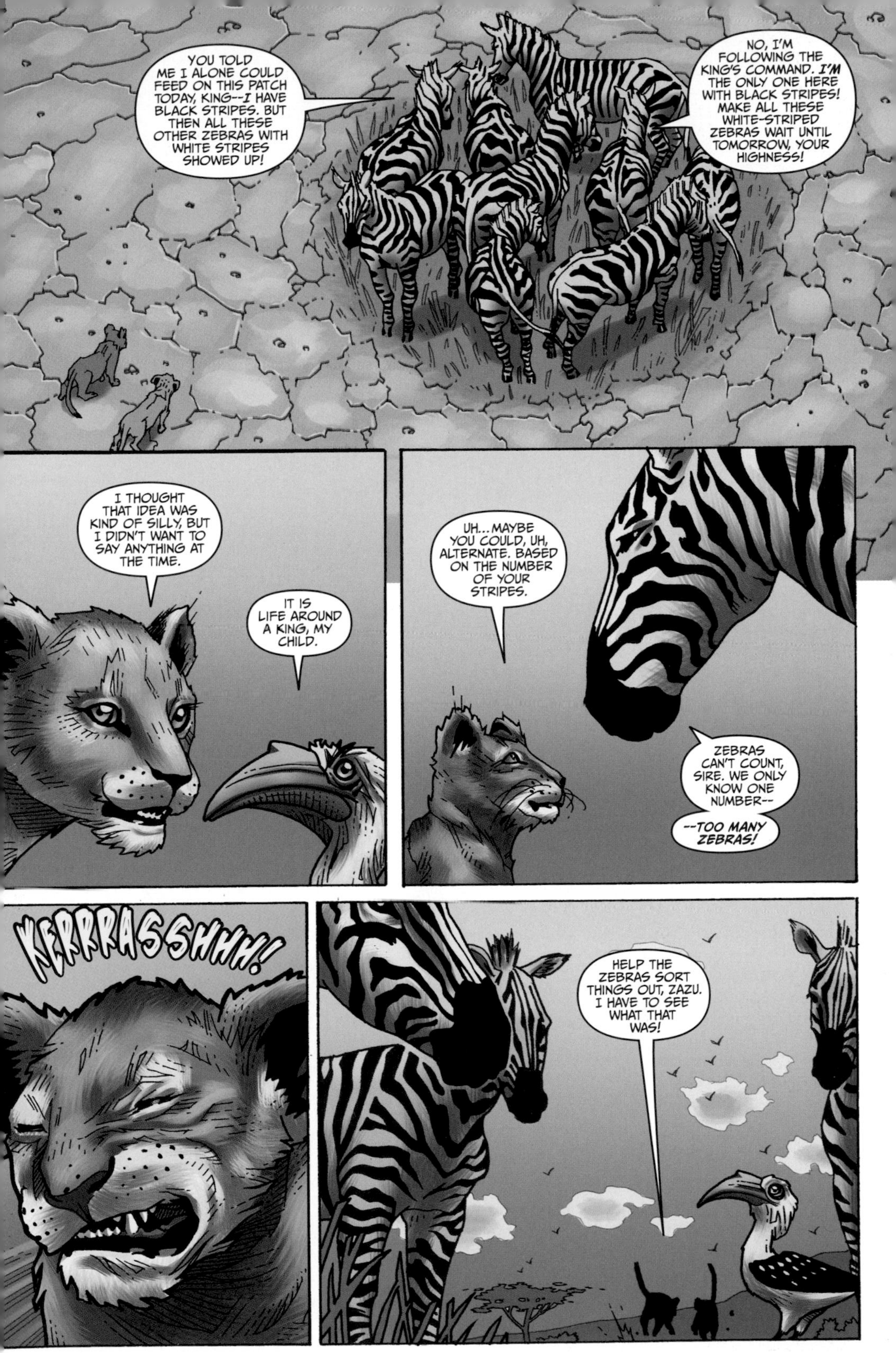
YOU TOLD ME I ALONE COULD FEED ON THIS PATCH TODAY, KING--I HAVE BLACK STRIPES. BUT THEN ALL THESE OTHER ZEBRAS WITH WHITE STRIPES SHOWED UP!
NO, I'M FOLLOWING THE KING'S COMMAND. I'M THE ONLY ONE HERE WITH BLACK STRIPES! MAKE ALL THESE WHITE-STRIPED ZEBRAS WAIT UNTIL TOMORROW, YOUR HIGHNESS!
I THOUGHT THAT IDEA WAS KIND OF SILLY, BUT I DIDN'T WANT TO SAY ANYTHING AT THE TIME.
IT IS LIFE AROUND A KING, MY CHILD.
UH...MAYBE YOU COULD, UH, ALTERNATE. BASED ON THE NUMBER OF YOUR STRIPES.
ZEBRAS CAN'T COUNT, SIRE. WE ONLY KNOW ONE NUMBER--
--TOO MANY ZEBRAS!
KERRRASSHHH!
HELP THE ZEBRAS SORT THINGS OUT, ZAZU. I HAVE TO SEE WHAT THAT WAS!

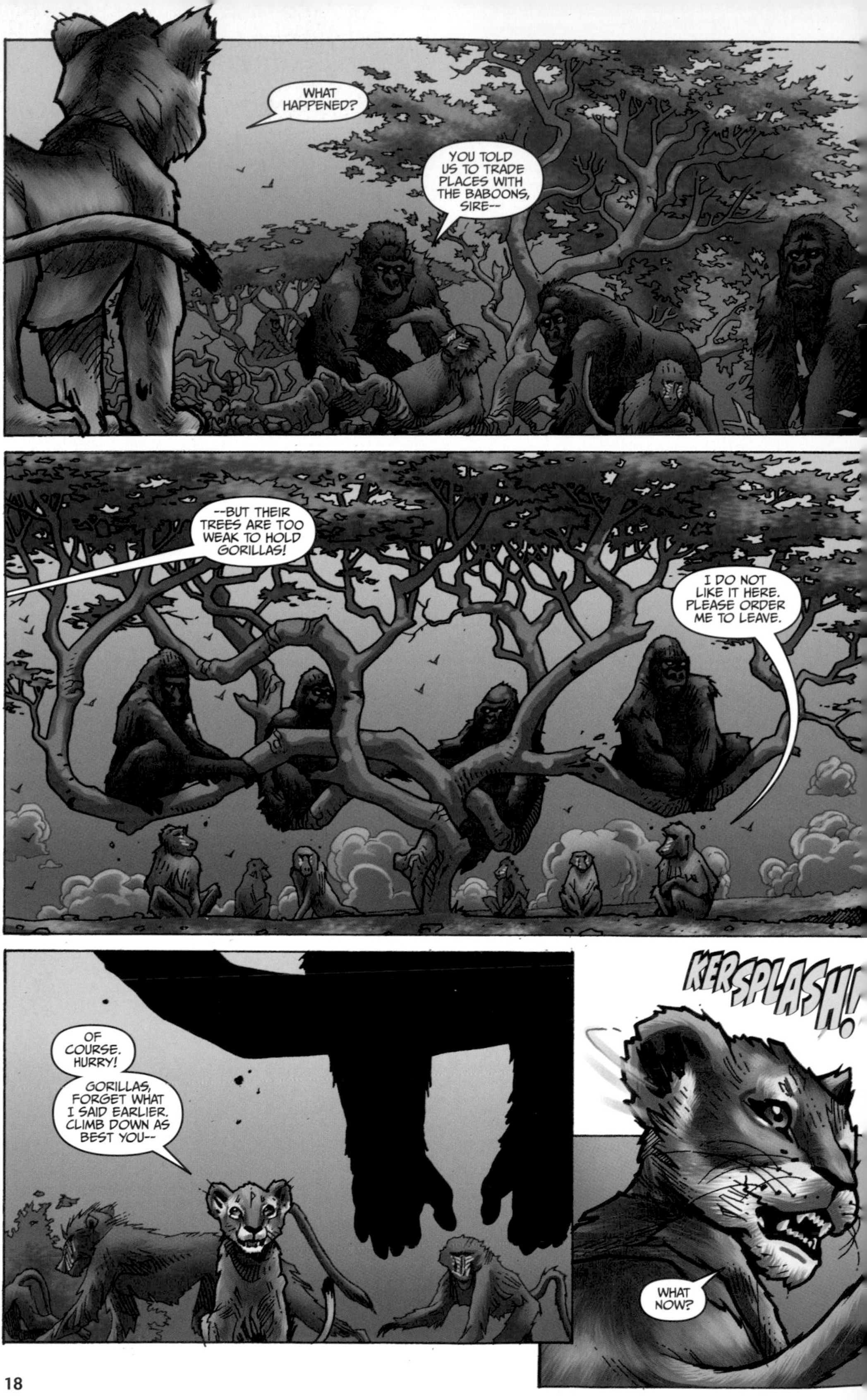
WHAT HAPPENED?
YOU TOLD US TO TRADE PLACES WITH THE BABOONS, SIRE--
--BUT THEIR TREES ARE TOO WEAK TO HOLD GORILLAS!
I DO NOT LIKE IT HERE. PLEASE ORDER ME TO LEAVE.
OF COURSE. HURRY!
GORILLAS, FORGET WHAT I SAID EARLIER. CLIMB DOWN AS BEST YOU--
KERSPLASH!
WHAT NOW?

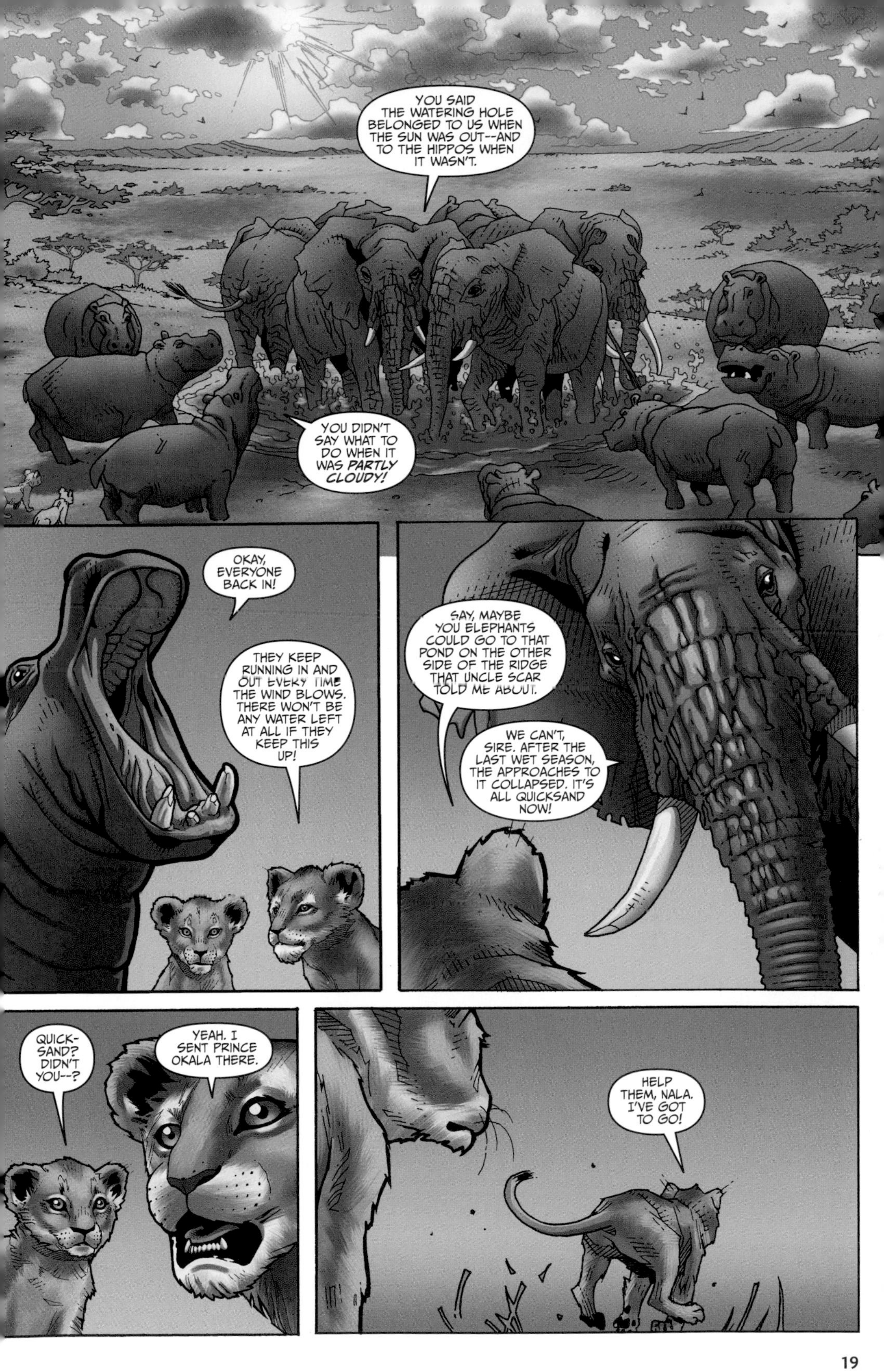
YOU SAID THE WATERING HOLE BELONGED TO US WHEN THE SUN WAS OUT--AND TO THE HIPPOS WHEN IT WASN'T.
YOU DIDN'T SAY WHAT TO DO WHEN IT WAS *PARTLY CLOUDY!*
OKAY, EVERYONE BACK IN!
THEY KEEP RUNNING IN AND OUT EVERY TIME THE WIND BLOWS. THERE WON'T BE ANY WATER LEFT AT ALL IF THEY KEEP THIS UP!
SAY, MAYBE YOU ELEPHANTS COULD GO TO THAT POND ON THE OTHER SIDE OF THE RIDGE THAT UNCLE SCAR TOLD ME ABOUT.
WE CAN'T, SIRE. AFTER THE LAST WET SEASON, THE APPROACHES TO IT COLLAPSED. IT'S ALL QUICKSAND NOW!
QUICK-SAND? DIDN'T YOU--?
YEAH. I SENT PRINCE OKALA THERE.
HELP THEM, NALA. I'VE GOT TO GO!

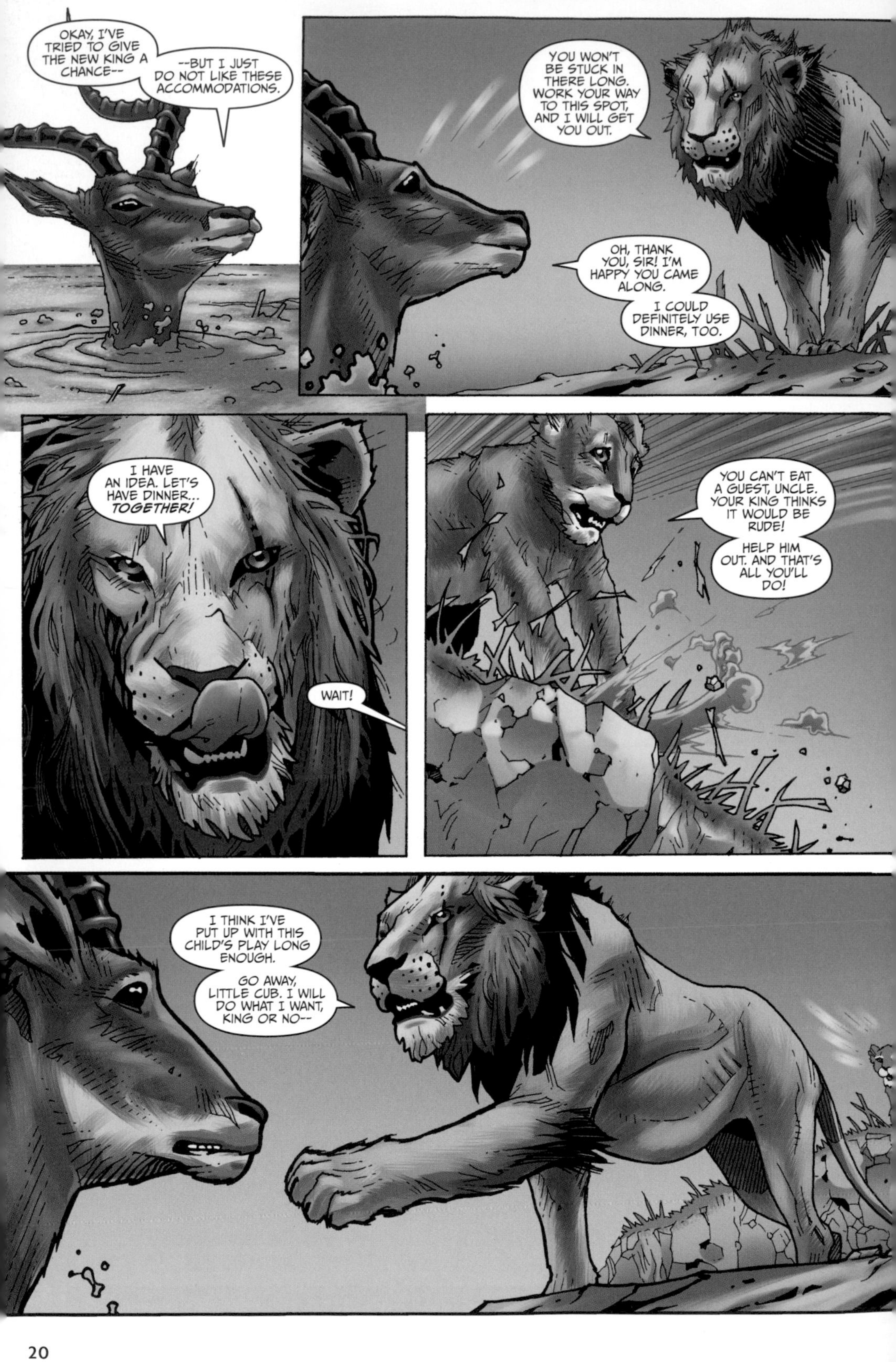
OKAY, I'VE TRIED TO GIVE THE NEW KING A CHANCE--
--BUT I JUST DO NOT LIKE THESE ACCOMMODATIONS.
YOU WON'T BE STUCK IN THERE LONG. WORK YOUR WAY TO THIS SPOT, AND I WILL GET YOU OUT.
OH, THANK YOU, SIR! I'M HAPPY YOU CAME ALONG.
I COULD DEFINITELY USE DINNER, TOO.
I HAVE AN IDEA. LET'S HAVE DINNER... TOGETHER!
WAIT!
YOU CAN'T EAT A GUEST, UNCLE. YOUR KING THINKS IT WOULD BE RUDE!
HELP HIM OUT. AND THAT'S ALL YOU'LL DO!
I THINK I'VE PUT UP WITH THIS CHILD'S PLAY LONG ENOUGH.
GO AWAY, LITTLE CUB. I WILL DO WHAT I WANT, KING OR NO--

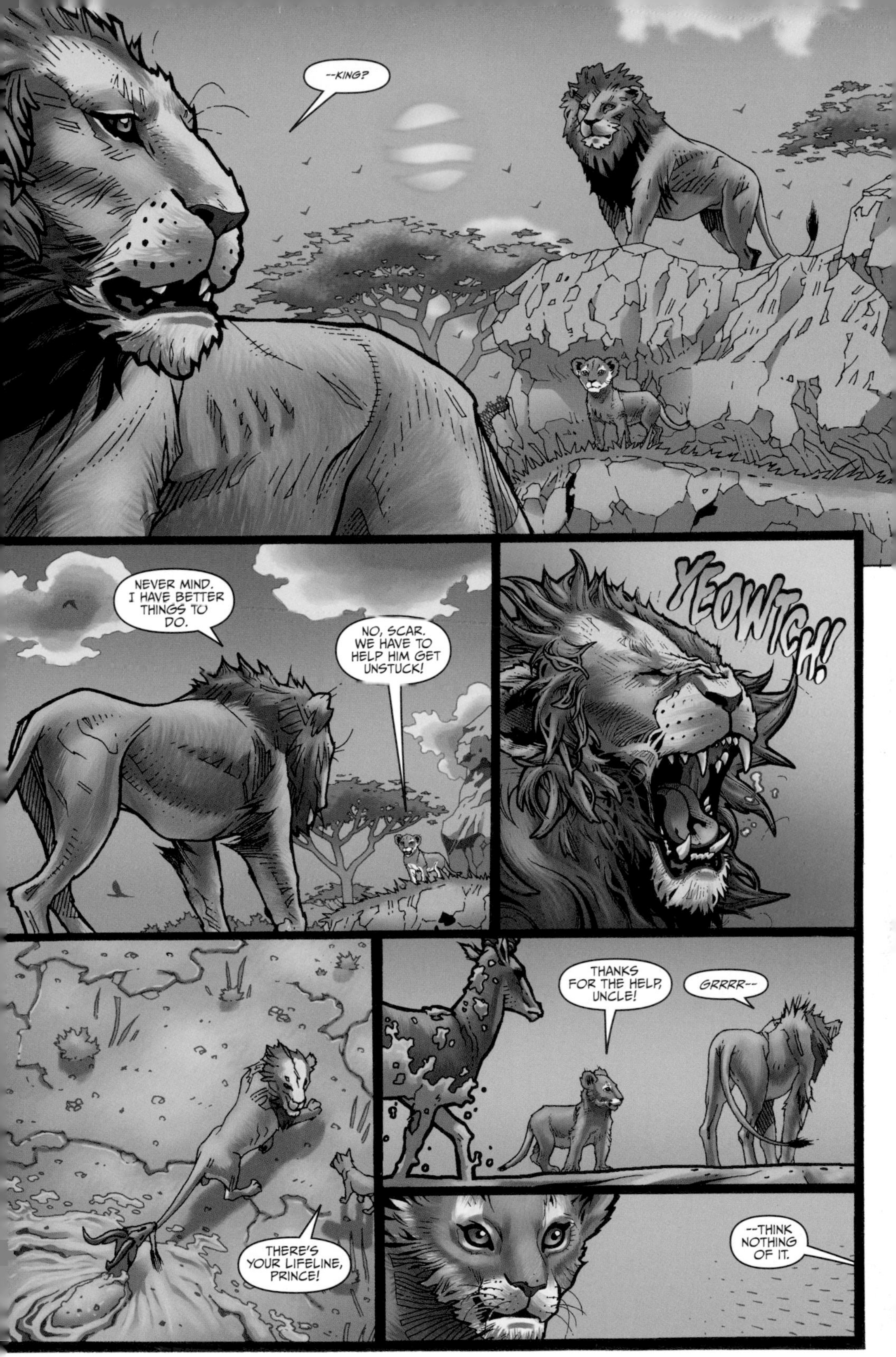
--KING?
NEVER MIND. I HAVE BETTER THINGS TO DO.
NO, SCAR. WE HAVE TO HELP HIM GET UNSTUCK!
YEOWTCH!
THERE'S YOUR LIFELINE, PRINCE!
THANKS FOR THE HELP, UNCLE!
GRRRR--
--THINK NOTHING OF IT.

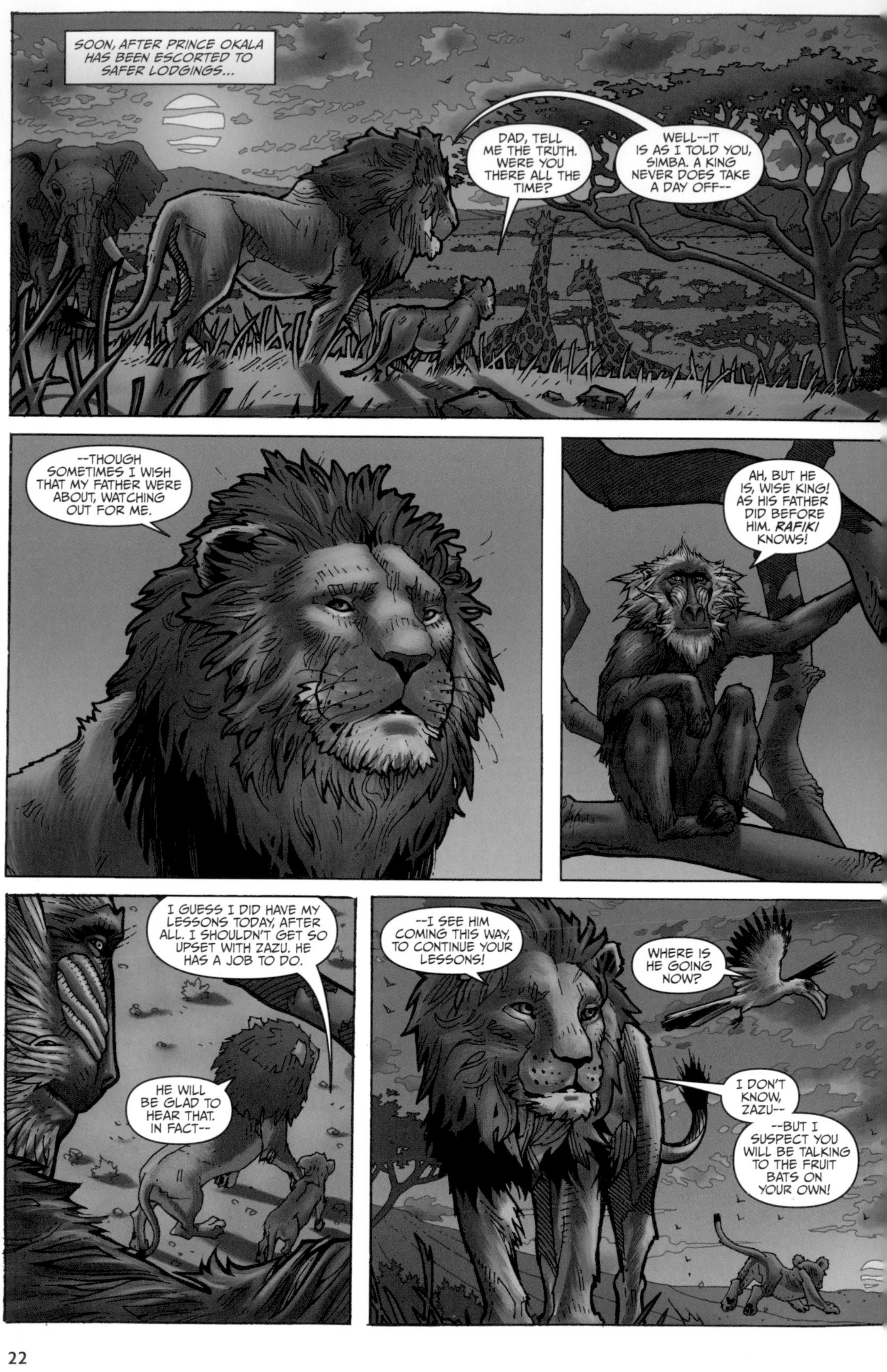
SOON, AFTER PRINCE OKALA HAS BEEN ESCORTED TO SAFER LODGINGS...
DAD, TELL ME THE TRUTH. WERE YOU THERE ALL THE TIME?
WELL--IT IS AS I TOLD YOU, SIMBA. A KING NEVER DOES TAKE A DAY OFF--
--THOUGH SOMETIMES I WISH THAT MY FATHER WERE ABOUT, WATCHING OUT FOR ME.
AH, BUT HE IS, WISE KING! AS HIS FATHER DID BEFORE HIM. RAFIKI KNOWS!
I GUESS I DID HAVE MY LESSONS TODAY, AFTER ALL. I SHOULDN'T GET SO UPSET WITH ZAZU. HE HAS A JOB TO DO.
HE WILL BE GLAD TO HEAR THAT. IN FACT--
--I SEE HIM COMING THIS WAY, TO CONTINUE YOUR LESSONS!
WHERE IS HE GOING NOW?
I DON'T KNOW, ZAZU--
--BUT I SUSPECT YOU WILL BE TALKING TO THE FRUIT BATS ON YOUR OWN!

KEEPER OF THE EGG

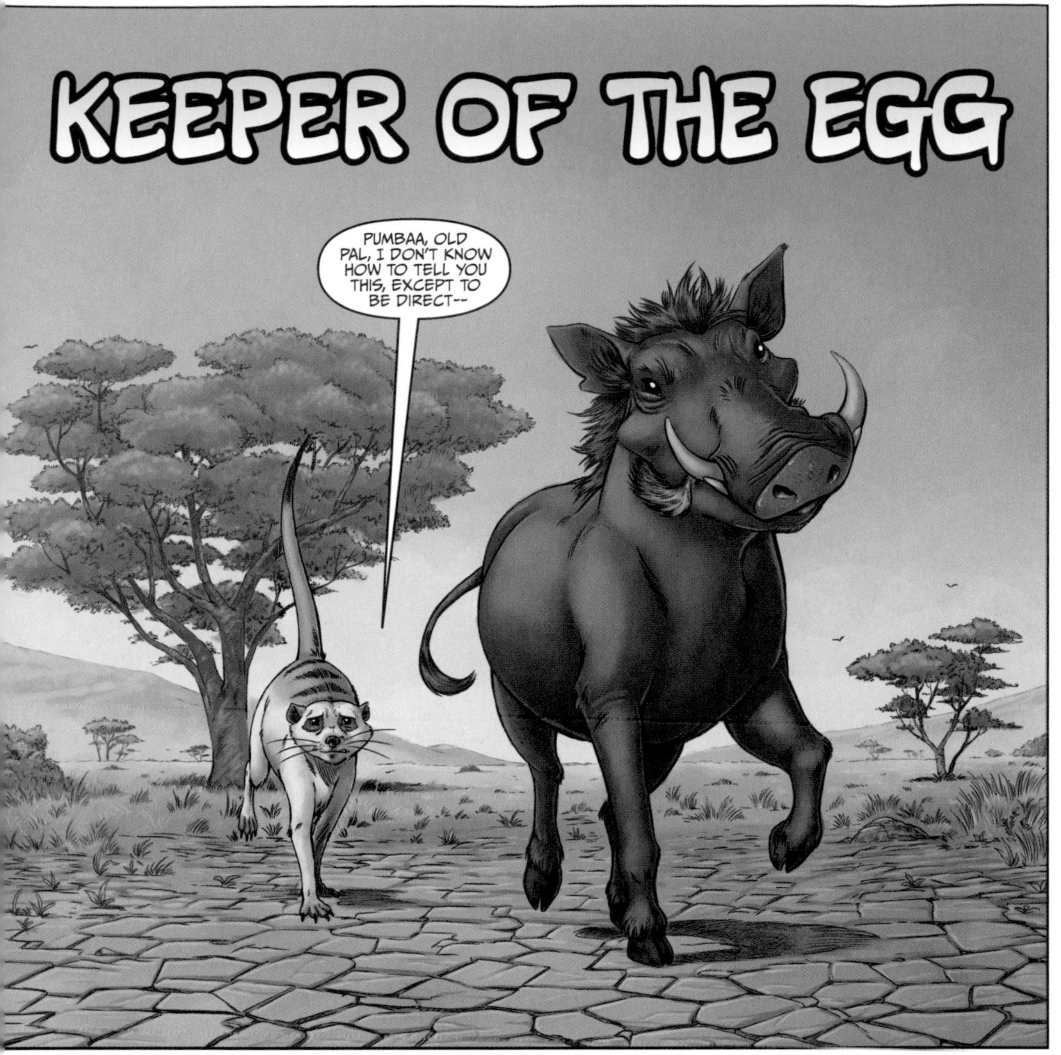
PUMBAA, OLD PAL, I DON'T KNOW HOW TO TELL YOU THIS, EXCEPT TO BE DIRECT--

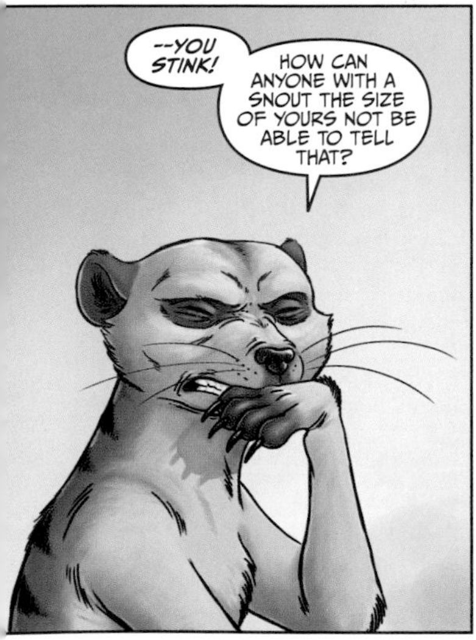
--YOU STINK!
HOW CAN ANYONE WITH A SNOUT THE SIZE OF YOURS NOT BE ABLE TO TELL THAT?

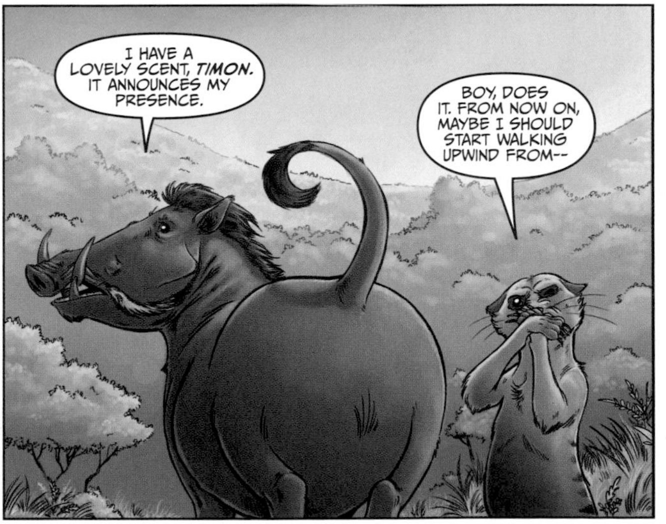
I HAVE A LOVELY SCENT, *TIMON.* IT ANNOUNCES MY PRESENCE.
BOY, DOES IT. FROM NOW ON, MAYBE I SHOULD START WALKING UPWIND FROM--

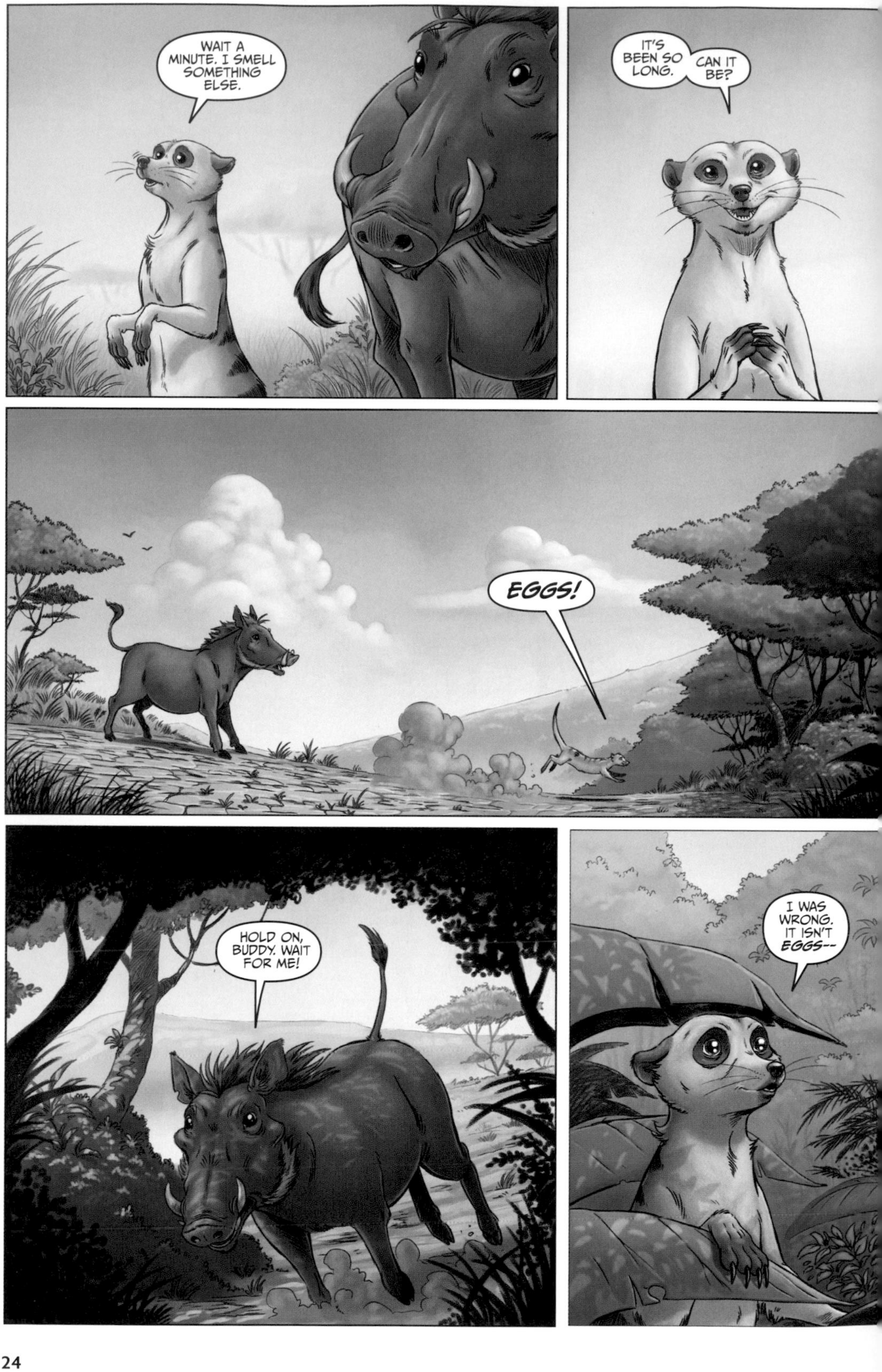
WAIT A MINUTE. I SMELL SOMETHING ELSE.
IT'S BEEN SO LONG.
CAN IT BE?
EGGS!
HOLD ON, BUDDY. WAIT FOR ME!
I WAS WRONG. IT ISN'T EGGS--

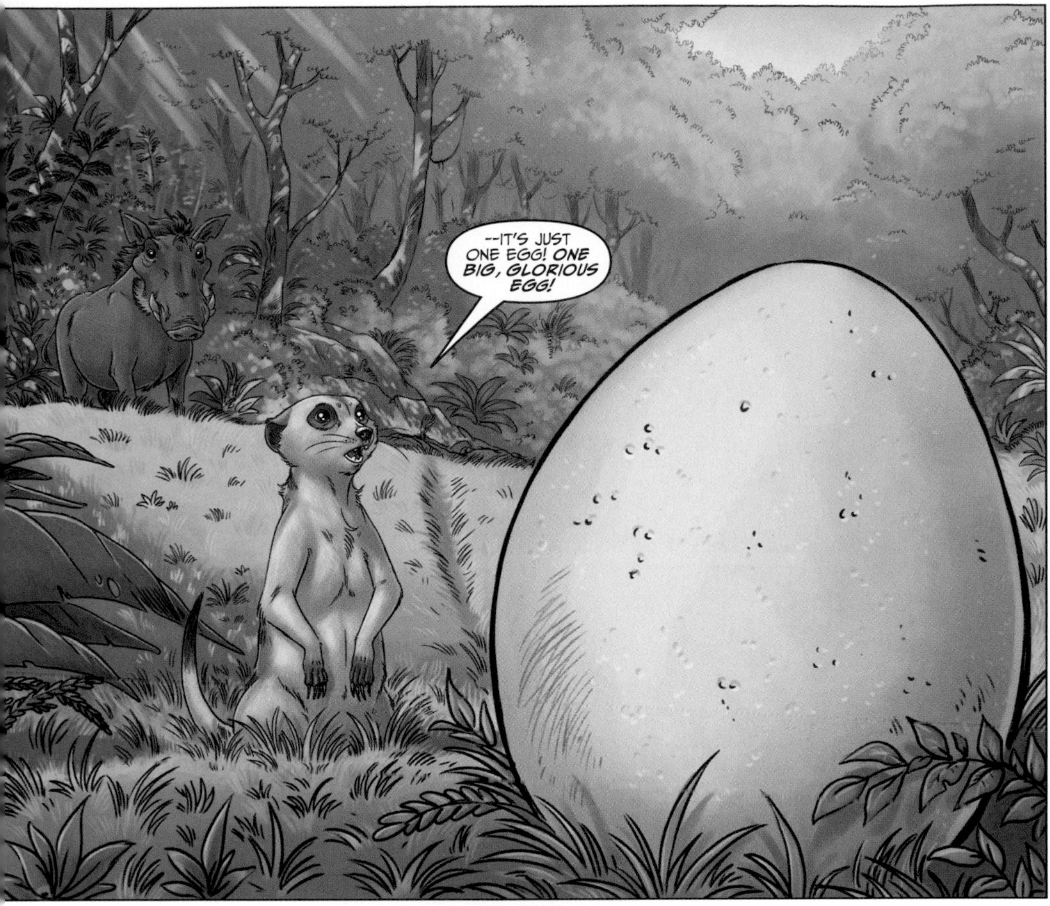
--IT'S JUST ONE EGG! ONE BIG, GLORIOUS EGG!

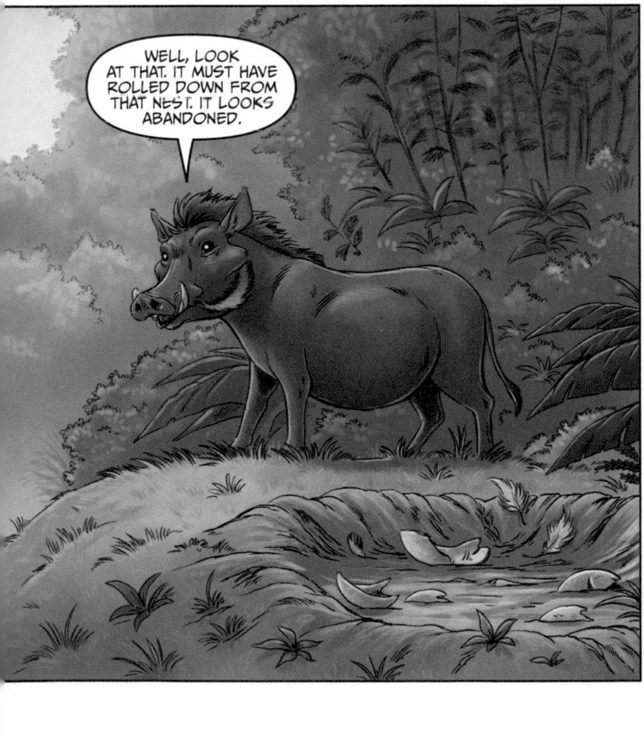
WELL, LOOK AT THAT. IT MUST HAVE ROLLED DOWN FROM THAT NEST. IT LOOKS ABANDONED.

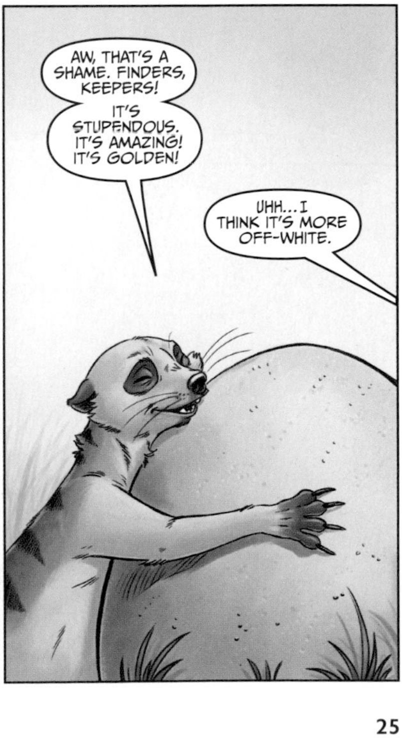
AW, THAT'S A SHAME. FINDERS, KEEPERS!
IT'S STUPENDOUS. IT'S AMAZING! IT'S GOLDEN!
UHH... I THINK IT'S MORE OFF-WHITE.

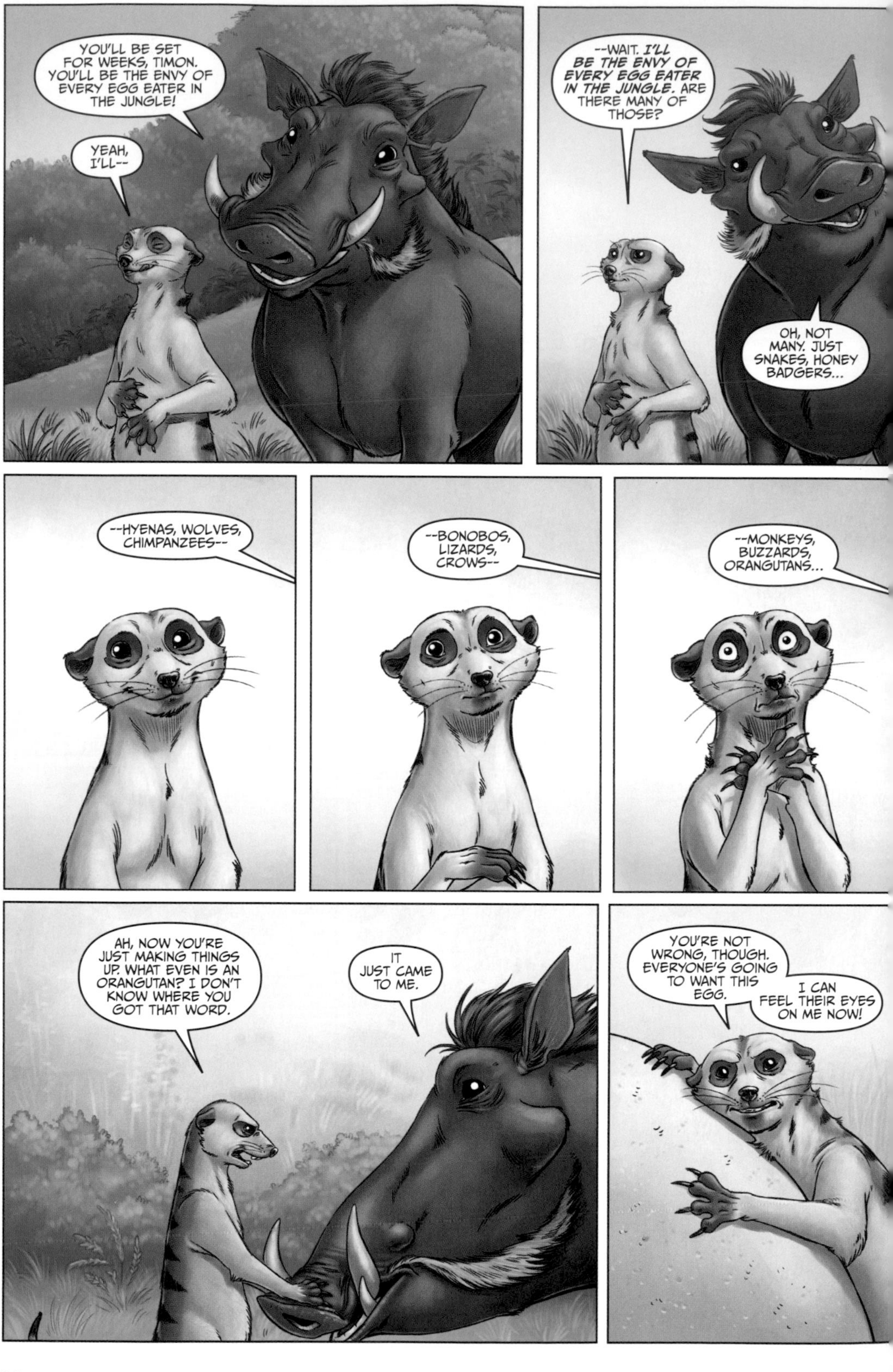
YOU'LL BE SET FOR WEEKS, TIMON. YOU'LL BE THE ENVY OF EVERY EGG EATER IN THE JUNGLE!
YEAH, I'LL--
--WAIT. *I'LL BE THE ENVY OF EVERY EGG EATER IN THE JUNGLE.* ARE THERE MANY OF THOSE?
OH, NOT MANY. JUST SNAKES, HONEY BADGERS...
--HYENAS, WOLVES, CHIMPANZEES--
--BONOBOS, LIZARDS, CROWS--
--MONKEYS, BUZZARDS, ORANGUTANS...
AH, NOW YOU'RE JUST MAKING THINGS UP. WHAT EVEN IS AN ORANGUTAN? I DON'T KNOW WHERE YOU GOT THAT WORD.
IT JUST CAME TO ME.
YOU'RE NOT WRONG, THOUGH. EVERYONE'S GOING TO WANT THIS EGG.
I CAN FEEL THEIR EYES ON ME NOW!

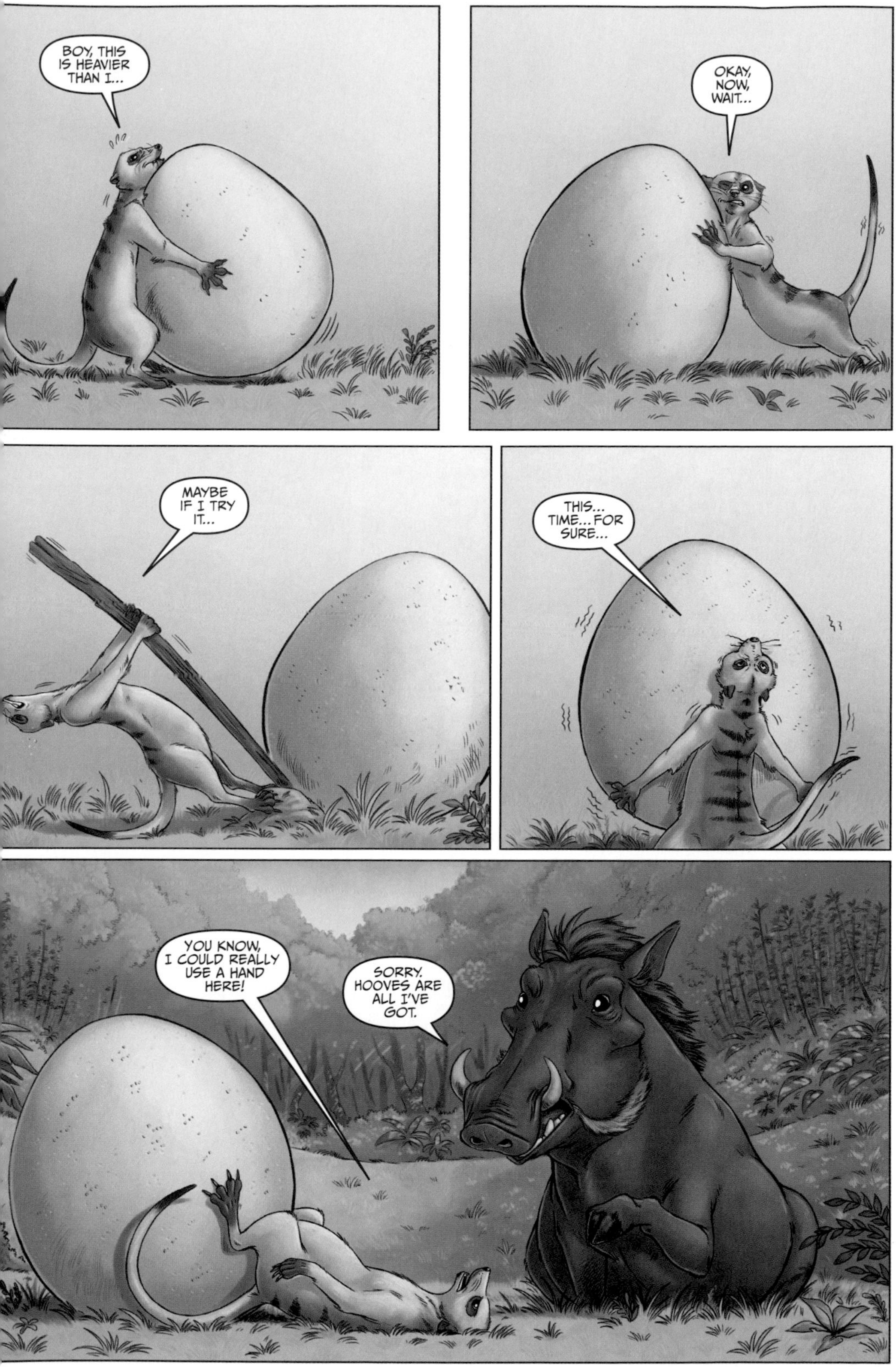
BOY, THIS IS HEAVIER THAN I...
OKAY, NOW, WAIT...
MAYBE IF I TRY IT...
THIS... TIME...FOR SURE...
YOU KNOW, I COULD REALLY USE A HAND HERE!
SORRY. HOOVES ARE ALL I'VE GOT.

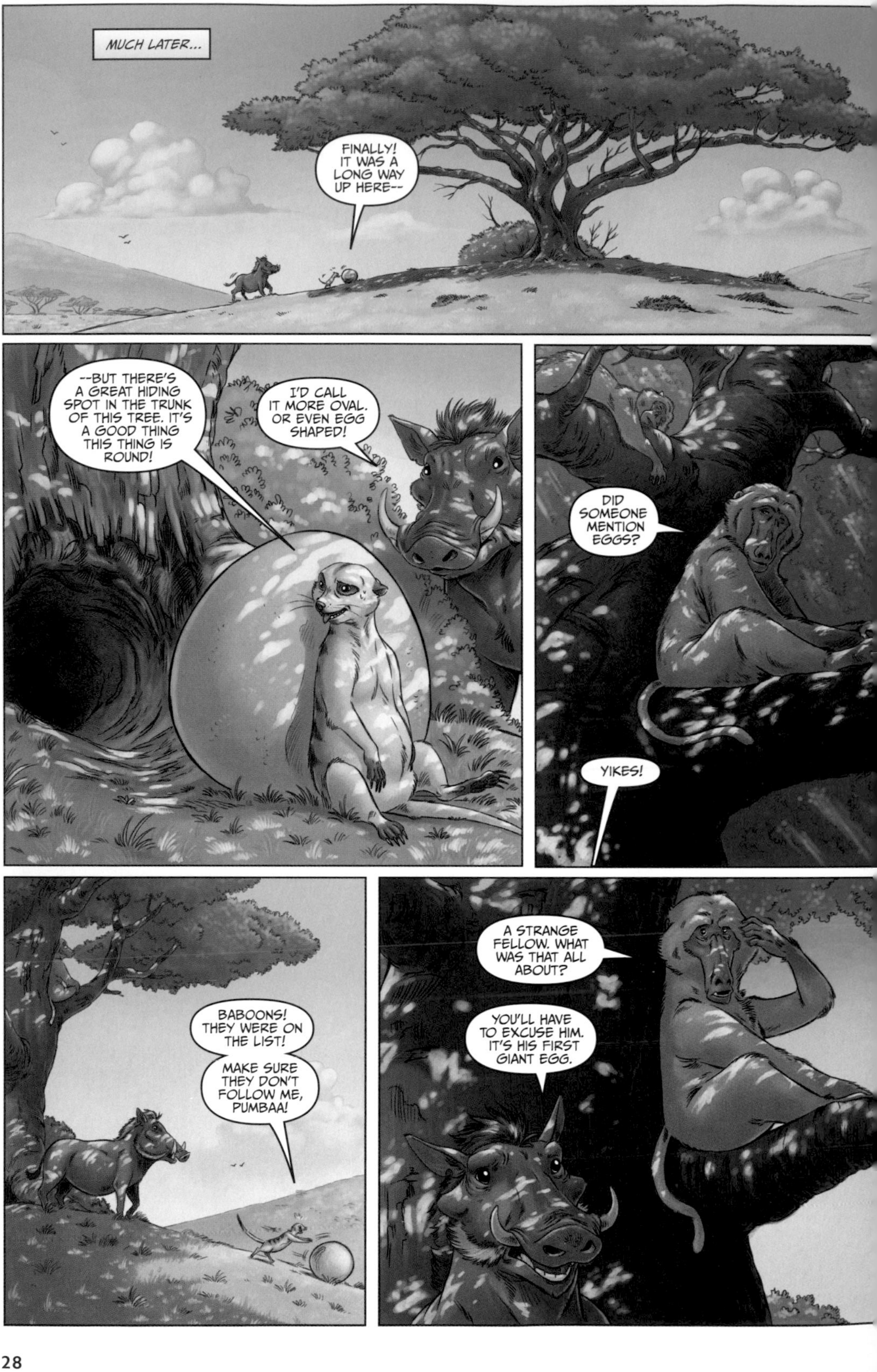
MUCH LATER...
FINALLY! IT WAS A LONG WAY UP HERE--
--BUT THERE'S A GREAT HIDING SPOT IN THE TRUNK OF THIS TREE. IT'S A GOOD THING THIS THING IS ROUND!
I'D CALL IT MORE OVAL. OR EVEN EGG SHAPED!
DID SOMEONE MENTION EGGS?
YIKES!
BABOONS! THEY WERE ON THE LIST!
MAKE SURE THEY DON'T FOLLOW ME, PUMBAA!
A STRANGE FELLOW. WHAT WAS THAT ALL ABOUT?
YOU'LL HAVE TO EXCUSE HIM. IT'S HIS FIRST GIANT EGG.

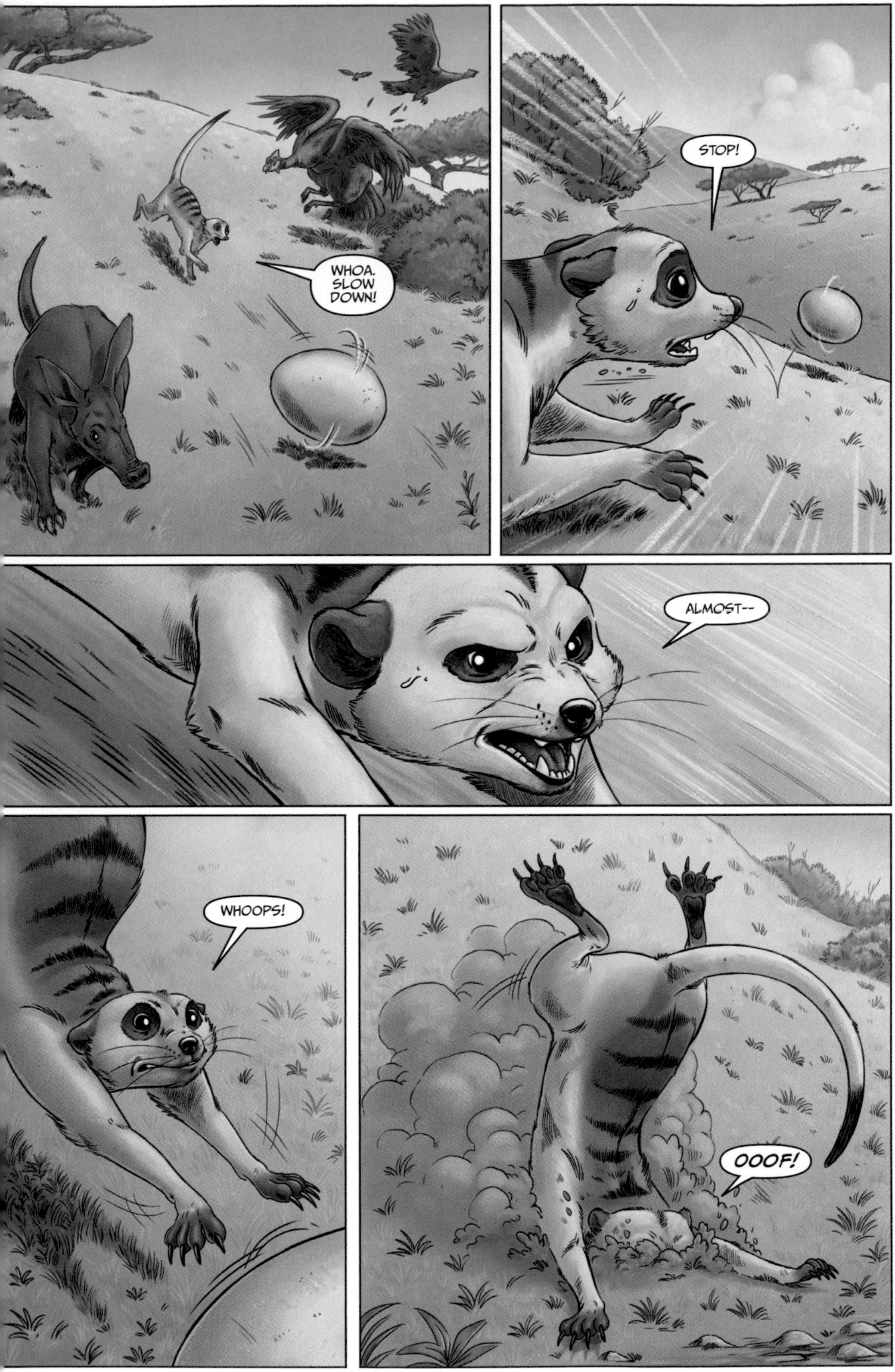
WHOA. SLOW DOWN!
STOP!
ALMOST--
WHOOPS!
OOOF!

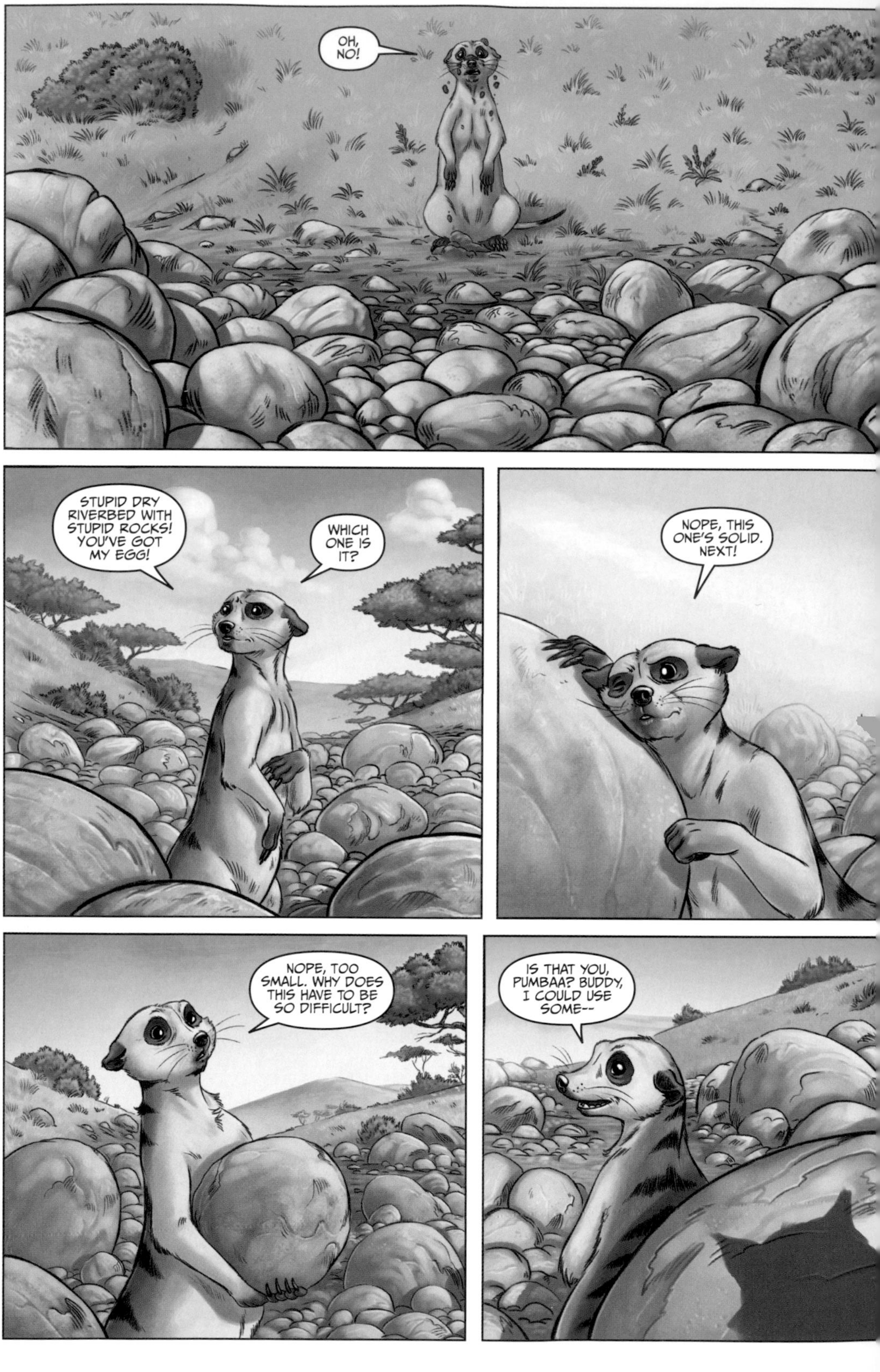
OH, NO!
STUPID DRY RIVERBED WITH STUPID ROCKS! YOU'VE GOT MY EGG!
WHICH ONE IS IT?
NOPE, THIS ONE'S SOLID. NEXT!
NOPE, TOO SMALL. WHY DOES THIS HAVE TO BE SO DIFFICULT?
IS THAT YOU, PUMBAA? BUDDY, I COULD USE SOME--

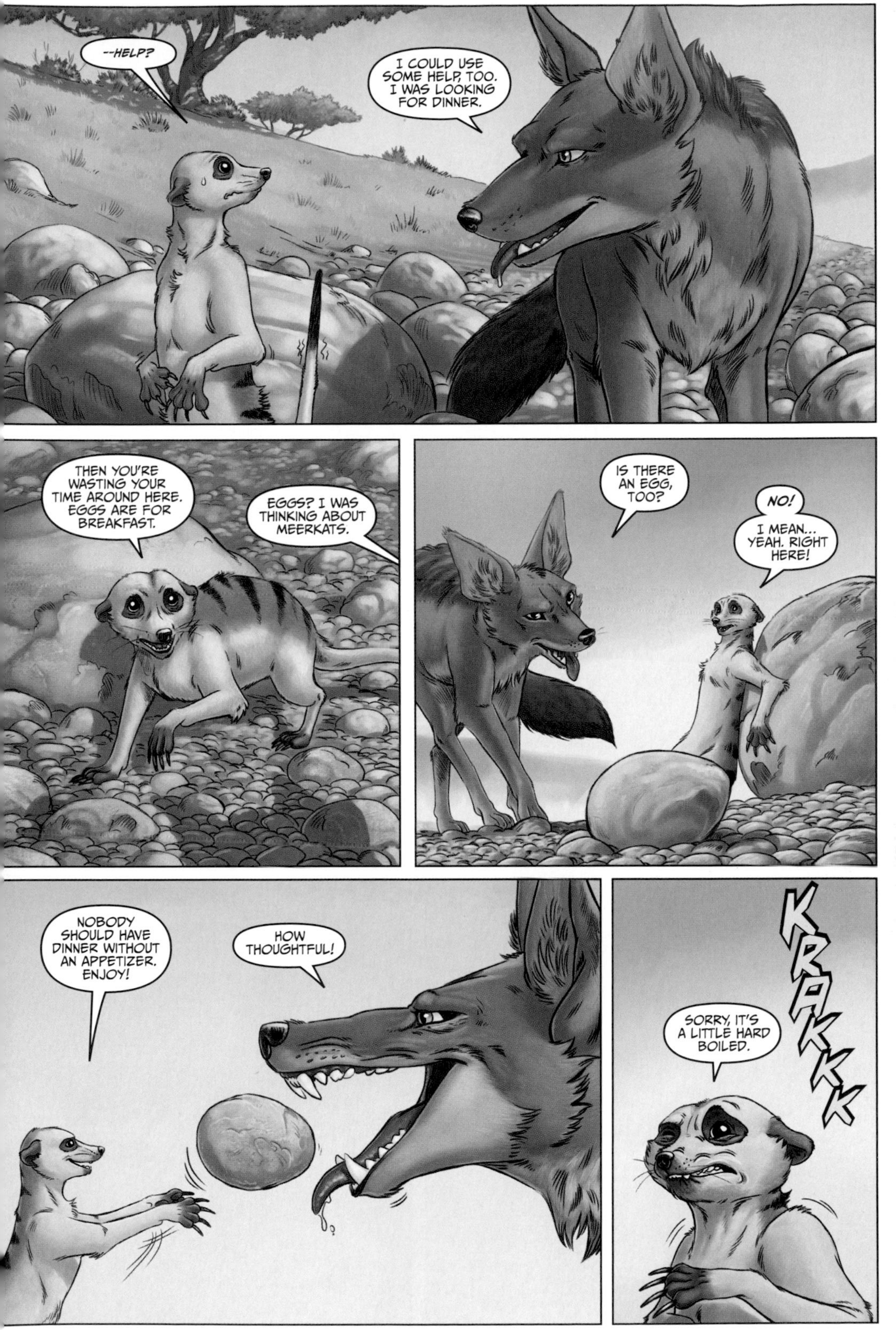
--HELP?
I COULD USE SOME HELP, TOO. I WAS LOOKING FOR DINNER.
THEN YOU'RE WASTING YOUR TIME AROUND HERE. EGGS ARE FOR BREAKFAST.
EGGS? I WAS THINKING ABOUT MEERKATS.
IS THERE AN EGG, TOO?
NO!
I MEAN... YEAH. RIGHT HERE!
NOBODY SHOULD HAVE DINNER WITHOUT AN APPETIZER. ENJOY!
HOW THOUGHTFUL!
KRAKKK
SORRY, IT'S A LITTLE HARD BOILED.

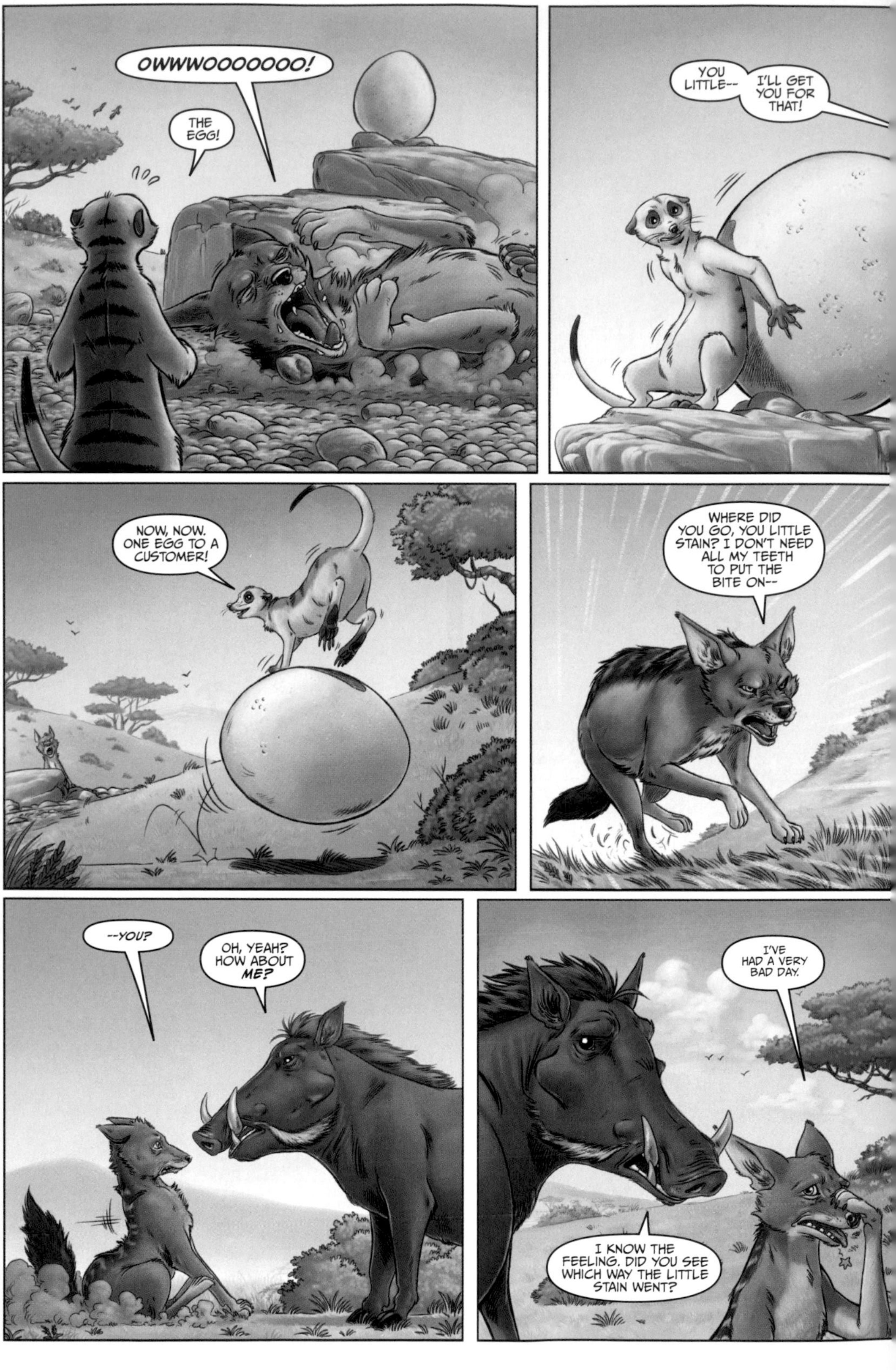
THE EGG!
OWWWOOOOOOO!
YOU LITTLE--
I'LL GET YOU FOR THAT!
NOW, NOW. ONE EGG TO A CUSTOMER!
WHERE DID YOU GO, YOU LITTLE STAIN? I DON'T NEED ALL MY TEETH TO PUT THE BITE ON--
--YOU?
OH, YEAH? HOW ABOUT ME?
I'VE HAD A VERY BAD DAY.
I KNOW THE FEELING. DID YOU SEE WHICH WAY THE LITTLE STAIN WENT?

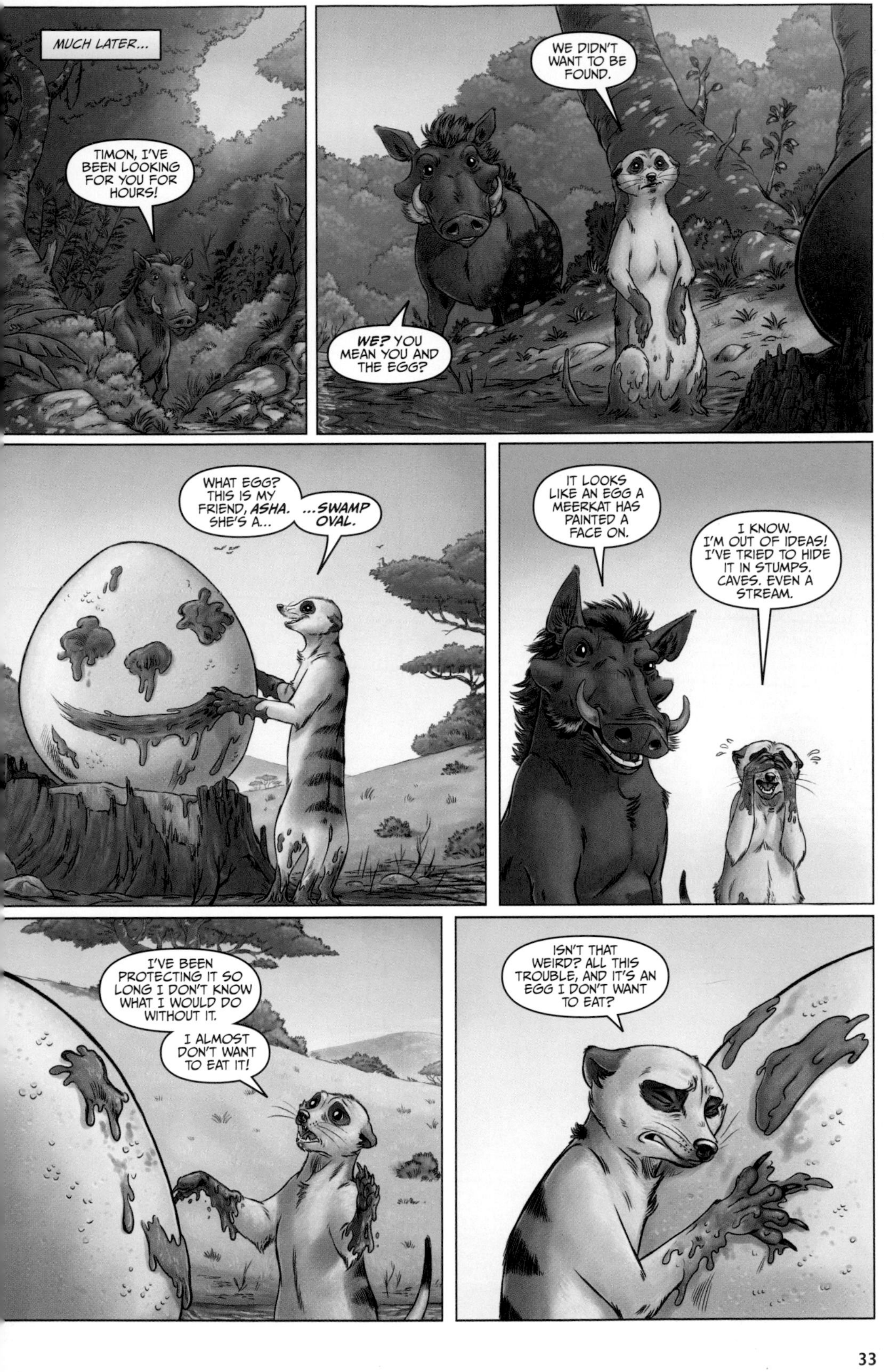
MUCH LATER...
TIMON, I'VE BEEN LOOKING FOR YOU FOR HOURS!
WE DIDN'T WANT TO BE FOUND.
WE? YOU MEAN YOU AND THE EGG?
WHAT EGG? THIS IS MY FRIEND, ASHA. SHE'S A...
...SWAMP OVAL.
IT LOOKS LIKE AN EGG A MEERKAT HAS PAINTED A FACE ON.
I KNOW. I'M OUT OF IDEAS! I'VE TRIED TO HIDE IT IN STUMPS. CAVES. EVEN A STREAM.
I'VE BEEN PROTECTING IT SO LONG I DON'T KNOW WHAT I WOULD DO WITHOUT IT.
I ALMOST DON'T WANT TO EAT IT!
ISN'T THAT WEIRD? ALL THIS TROUBLE, AND IT'S AN EGG I DON'T WANT TO EAT?

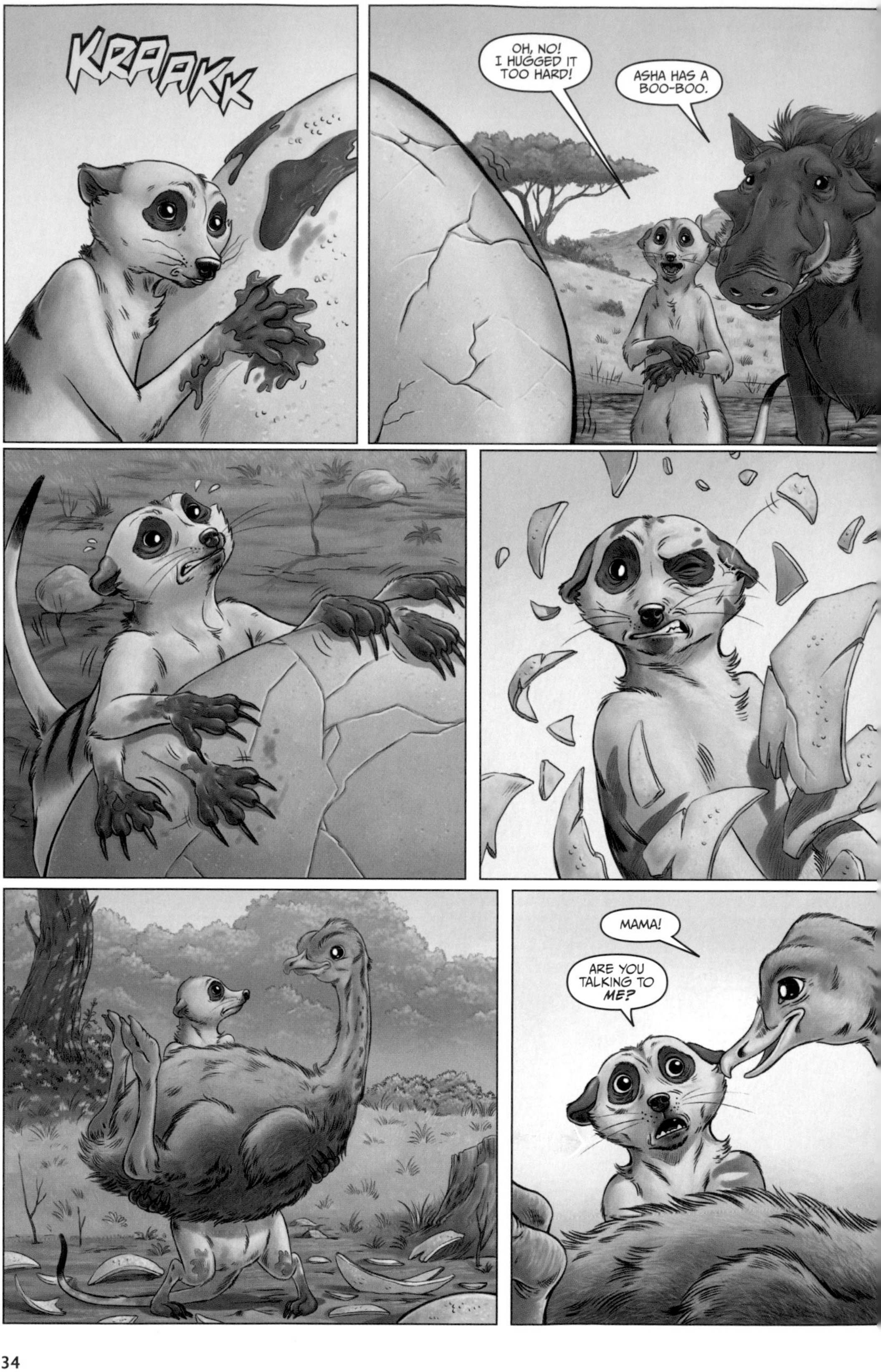
KRAAKK
OH, NO! I HUGGED IT TOO HARD!
ASHA HAS A BOO-BOO.
MAMA!
ARE YOU TALKING TO *ME?*

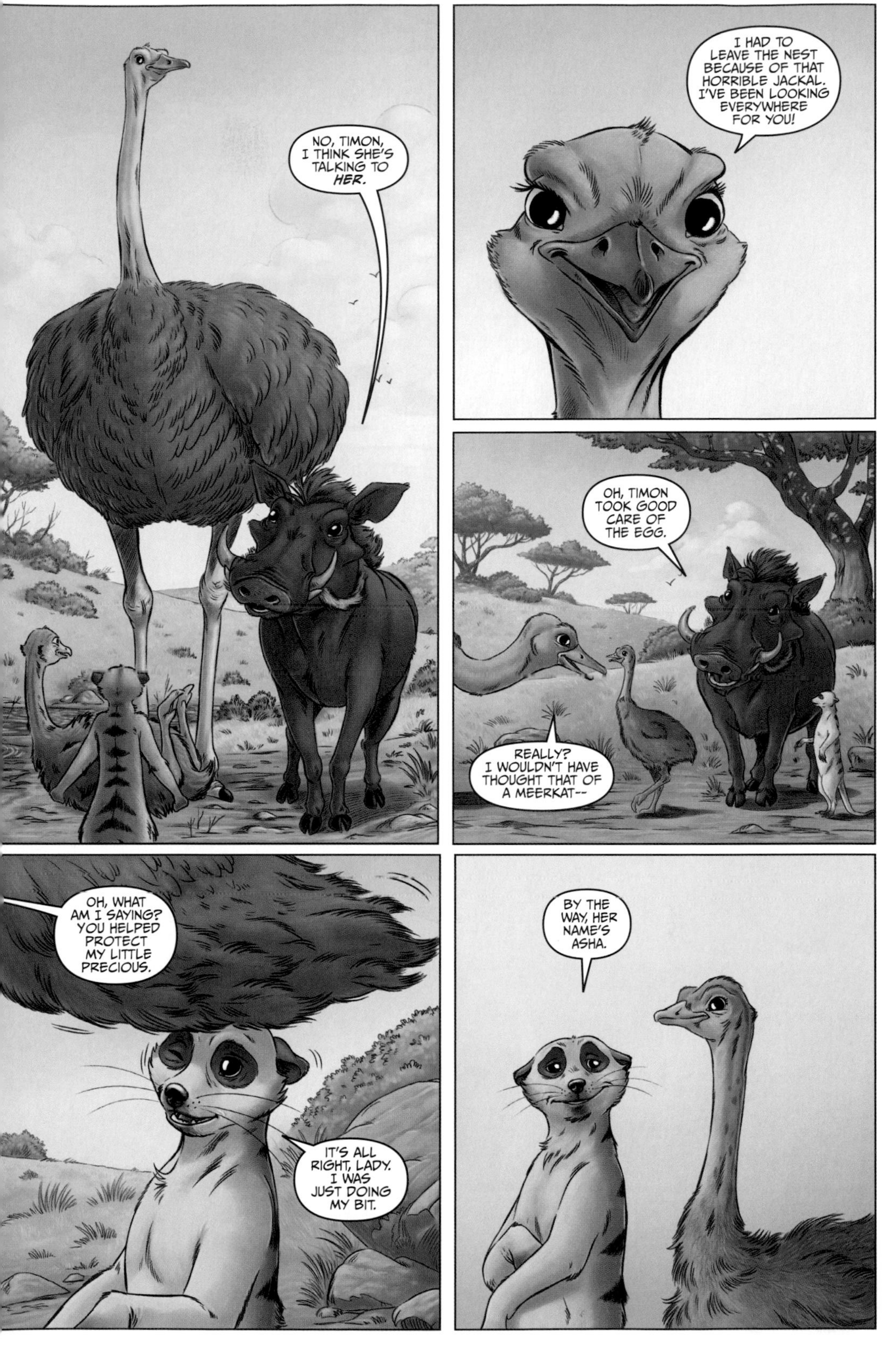

NO, TIMON, I THINK SHE'S TALKING TO HER.
I HAD TO LEAVE THE NEST BECAUSE OF THAT HORRIBLE JACKAL. I'VE BEEN LOOKING EVERYWHERE FOR YOU!
OH, TIMON TOOK GOOD CARE OF THE EGG.
REALLY? I WOULDN'T HAVE THOUGHT THAT OF A MEERKAT--
OH, WHAT AM I SAYING? YOU HELPED PROTECT MY LITTLE PRECIOUS.
IT'S ALL RIGHT, LADY. I WAS JUST DOING MY BIT.
BY THE WAY, HER NAME'S ASHA.

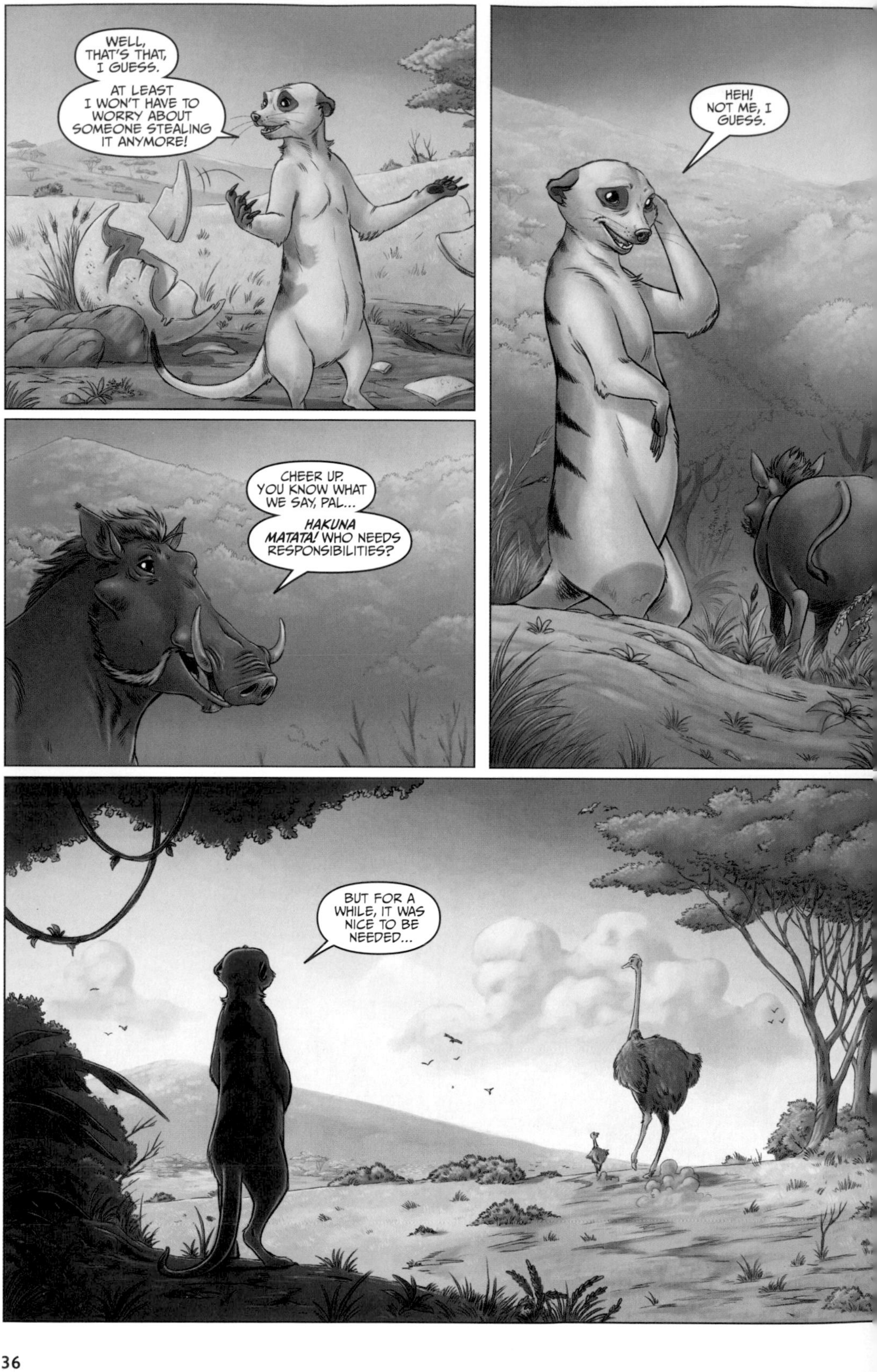
WELL, THAT'S THAT, I GUESS.
AT LEAST I WON'T HAVE TO WORRY ABOUT SOMEONE STEALING IT ANYMORE!
HEH! NOT ME, I GUESS.
CHEER UP. YOU KNOW WHAT WE SAY, PAL...
HAKUNA MATATA! WHO NEEDS RESPONSIBILITIES?
BUT FOR A WHILE, IT WAS NICE TO BE NEEDED...

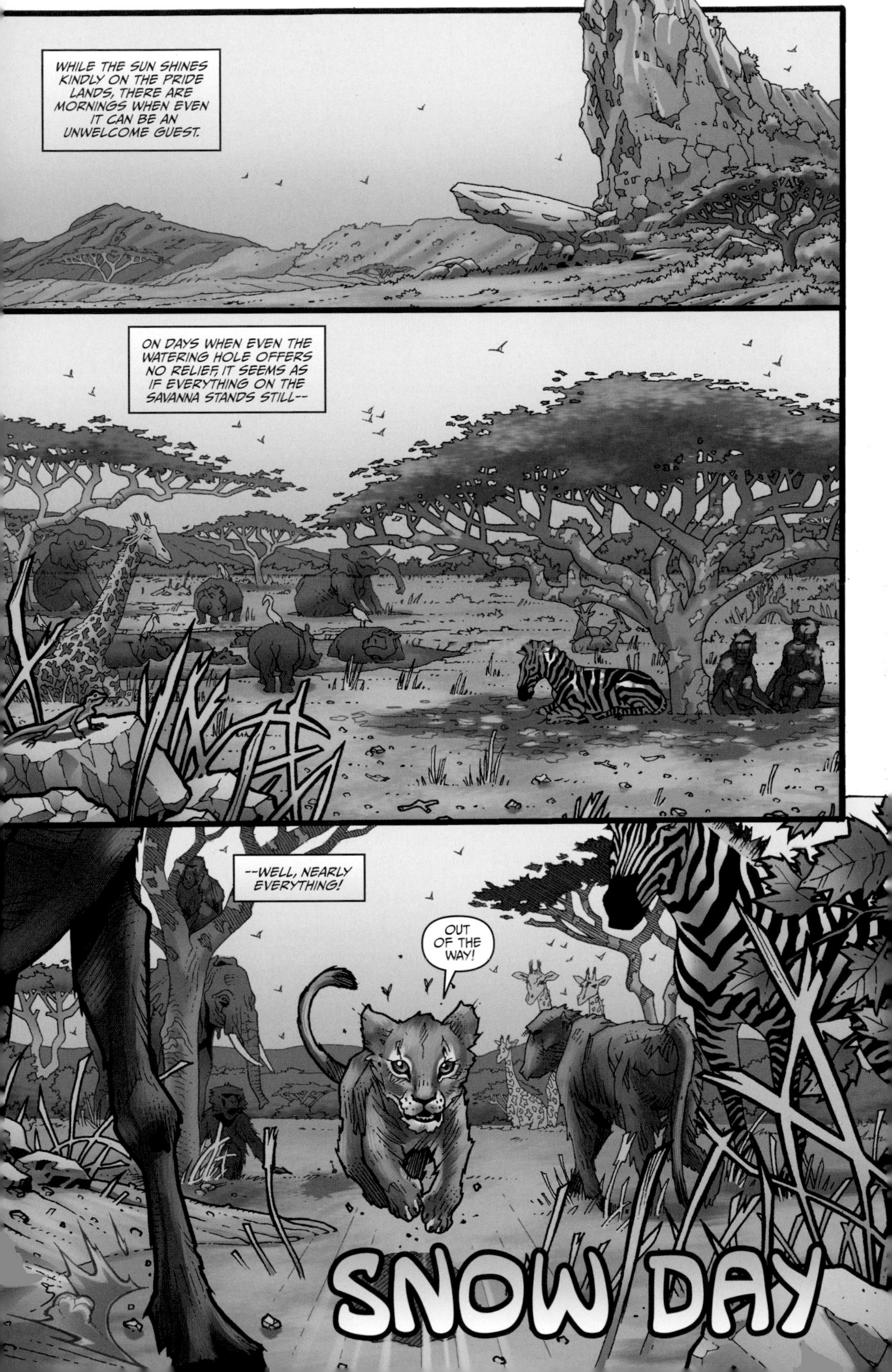
WHILE THE SUN SHINES KINDLY ON THE PRIDE LANDS, THERE ARE MORNINGS WHEN EVEN IT CAN BE AN UNWELCOME GUEST.
ON DAYS WHEN EVEN THE WATERING HOLE OFFERS NO RELIEF, IT SEEMS AS IF EVERYTHING ON THE SAVANNA STANDS STILL--
--WELL, NEARLY EVERYTHING!
OUT OF THE WAY!
SNOW DAY

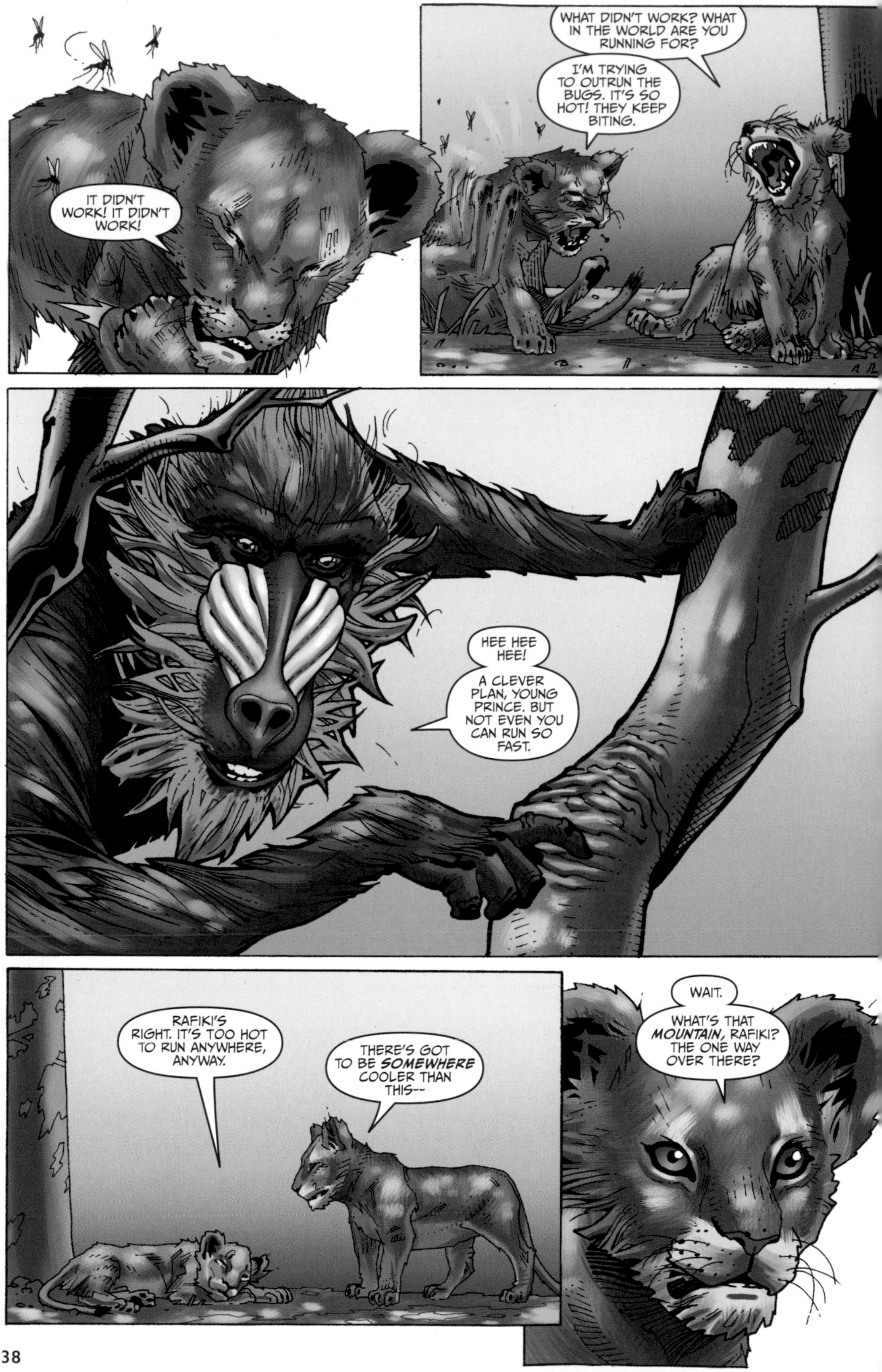
IT DIDN'T WORK! IT DIDN'T WORK!
WHAT DIDN'T WORK? WHAT IN THE WORLD ARE YOU RUNNING FOR?
I'M TRYING TO OUTRUN THE BUGS. IT'S SO HOT! THEY KEEP BITING.
HEE HEE HEE!
A CLEVER PLAN, YOUNG PRINCE. BUT NOT EVEN YOU CAN RUN SO FAST.
RAFIKI'S RIGHT. IT'S TOO HOT TO RUN ANYWHERE, ANYWAY.
THERE'S GOT TO BE ***SOMEWHERE*** COOLER THAN THIS--
WAIT.
WHAT'S THAT ***MOUNTAIN***, RAFIKI? THE ONE WAY OVER THERE?

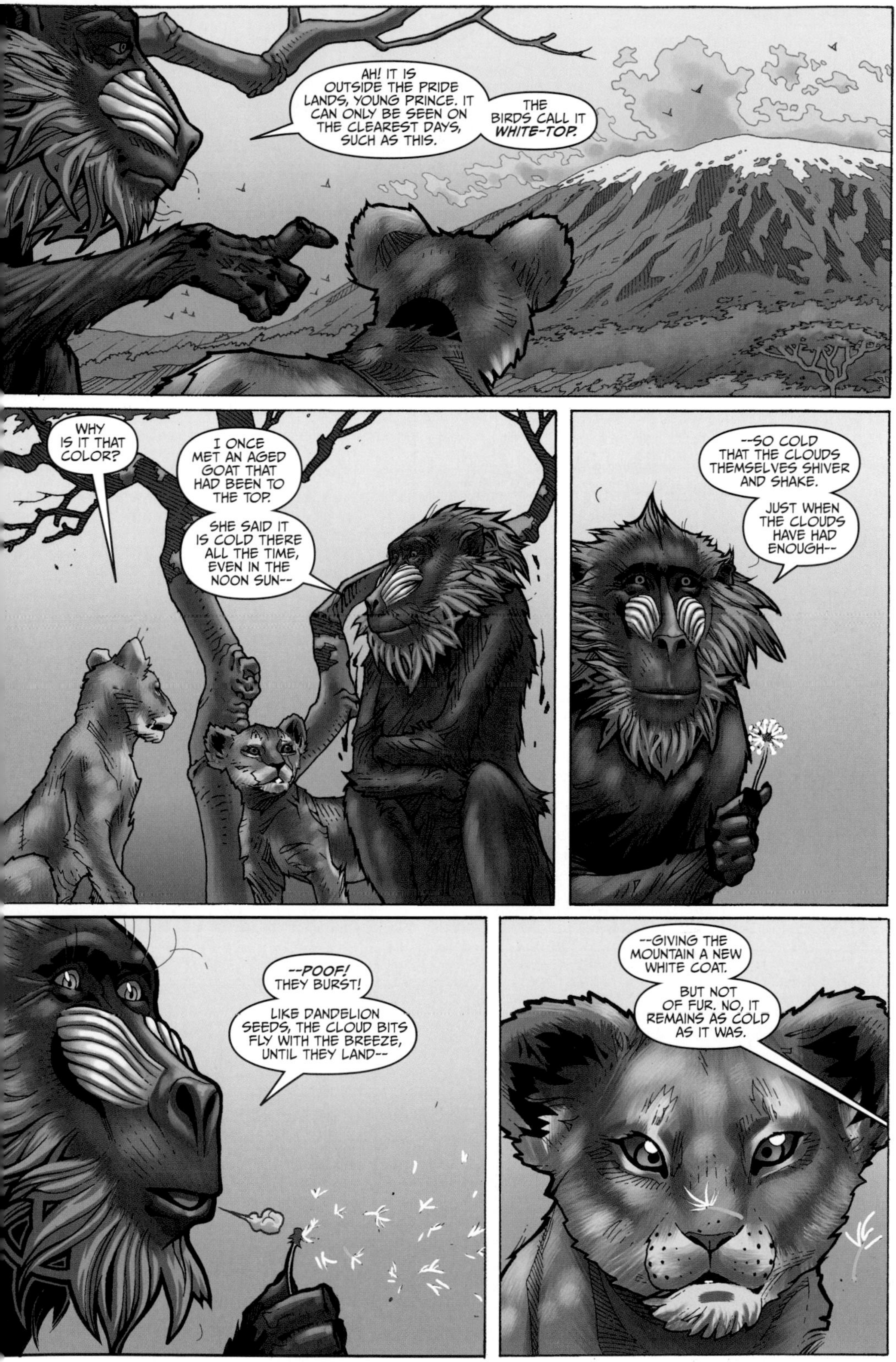
AH! IT IS OUTSIDE THE PRIDE LANDS, YOUNG PRINCE. IT CAN ONLY BE SEEN ON THE CLEAREST DAYS, SUCH AS THIS.
THE BIRDS CALL IT *WHITE-TOP.*
WHY IS IT THAT COLOR?
I ONCE MET AN AGED GOAT THAT HAD BEEN TO THE TOP.
SHE SAID IT IS COLD THERE ALL THE TIME, EVEN IN THE NOON SUN--
--SO COLD THAT THE CLOUDS THEMSELVES SHIVER AND SHAKE.
JUST WHEN THE CLOUDS HAVE HAD ENOUGH--
--POOF! THEY BURST!
LIKE DANDELION SEEDS, THE CLOUD BITS FLY WITH THE BREEZE, UNTIL THEY LAND--
--GIVING THE MOUNTAIN A NEW WHITE COAT.
BUT NOT OF FUR. NO, IT REMAINS AS COLD AS IT WAS.

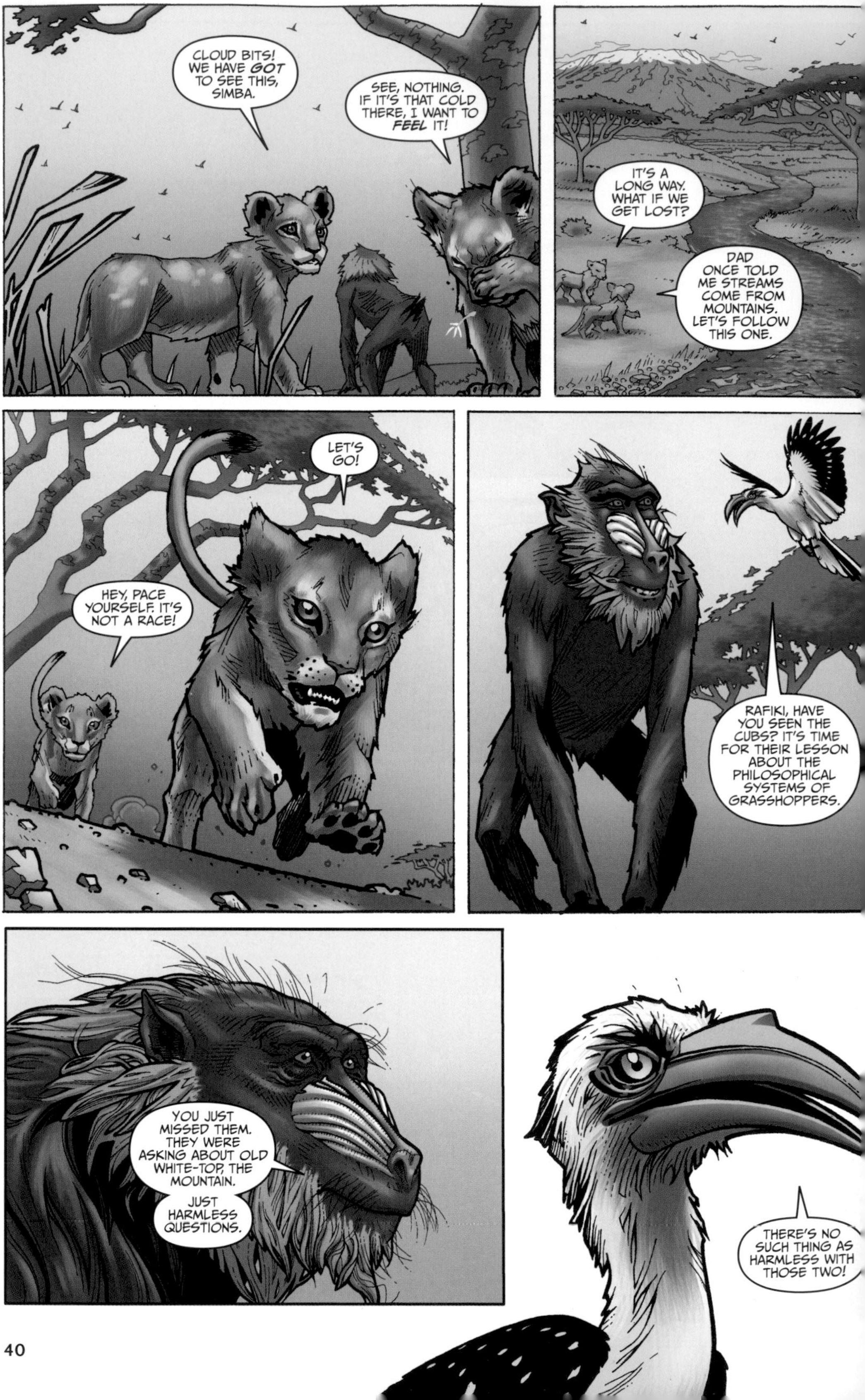
CLOUD BITS! WE HAVE GOT TO SEE THIS, SIMBA.
SEE, NOTHING. IF IT'S THAT COLD THERE, I WANT TO FEEL IT!
IT'S A LONG WAY. WHAT IF WE GET LOST?
DAD ONCE TOLD ME STREAMS COME FROM MOUNTAINS. LET'S FOLLOW THIS ONE.
LET'S GO!
HEY, PACE YOURSELF. IT'S NOT A RACE!
RAFIKI, HAVE YOU SEEN THE CUBS? IT'S TIME FOR THEIR LESSON ABOUT THE PHILOSOPHICAL SYSTEMS OF GRASSHOPPERS.
YOU JUST MISSED THEM. THEY WERE ASKING ABOUT OLD WHITE-TOP, THE MOUNTAIN.
JUST HARMLESS QUESTIONS.
THERE'S NO SUCH THING AS HARMLESS WITH THOSE TWO!

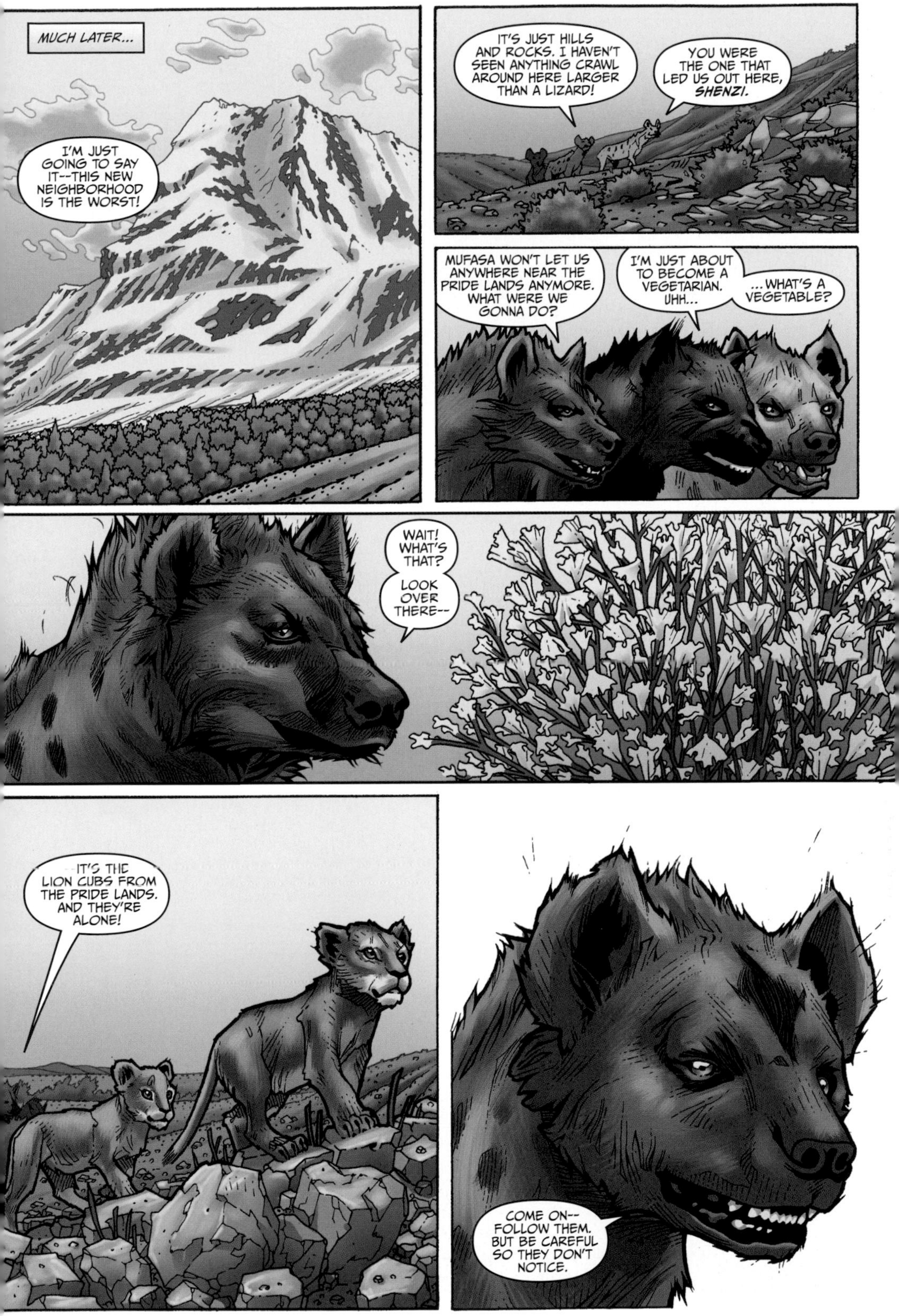
MUCH LATER...
I'M JUST GOING TO SAY IT--THIS NEW NEIGHBORHOOD IS THE WORST!
IT'S JUST HILLS AND ROCKS. I HAVEN'T SEEN ANYTHING CRAWL AROUND HERE LARGER THAN A LIZARD!
YOU WERE THE ONE THAT LED US OUT HERE, SHENZI.
MUFASA WON'T LET US ANYWHERE NEAR THE PRIDE LANDS ANYMORE. WHAT WERE WE GONNA DO?
I'M JUST ABOUT TO BECOME A VEGETARIAN. UHH...
...WHAT'S A VEGETABLE?
WAIT! WHAT'S THAT?
LOOK OVER THERE--
--IT'S THE LION CUBS FROM THE PRIDE LANDS. AND THEY'RE ALONE!
COME ON--FOLLOW THEM. BUT BE CAREFUL SO THEY DON'T NOTICE.

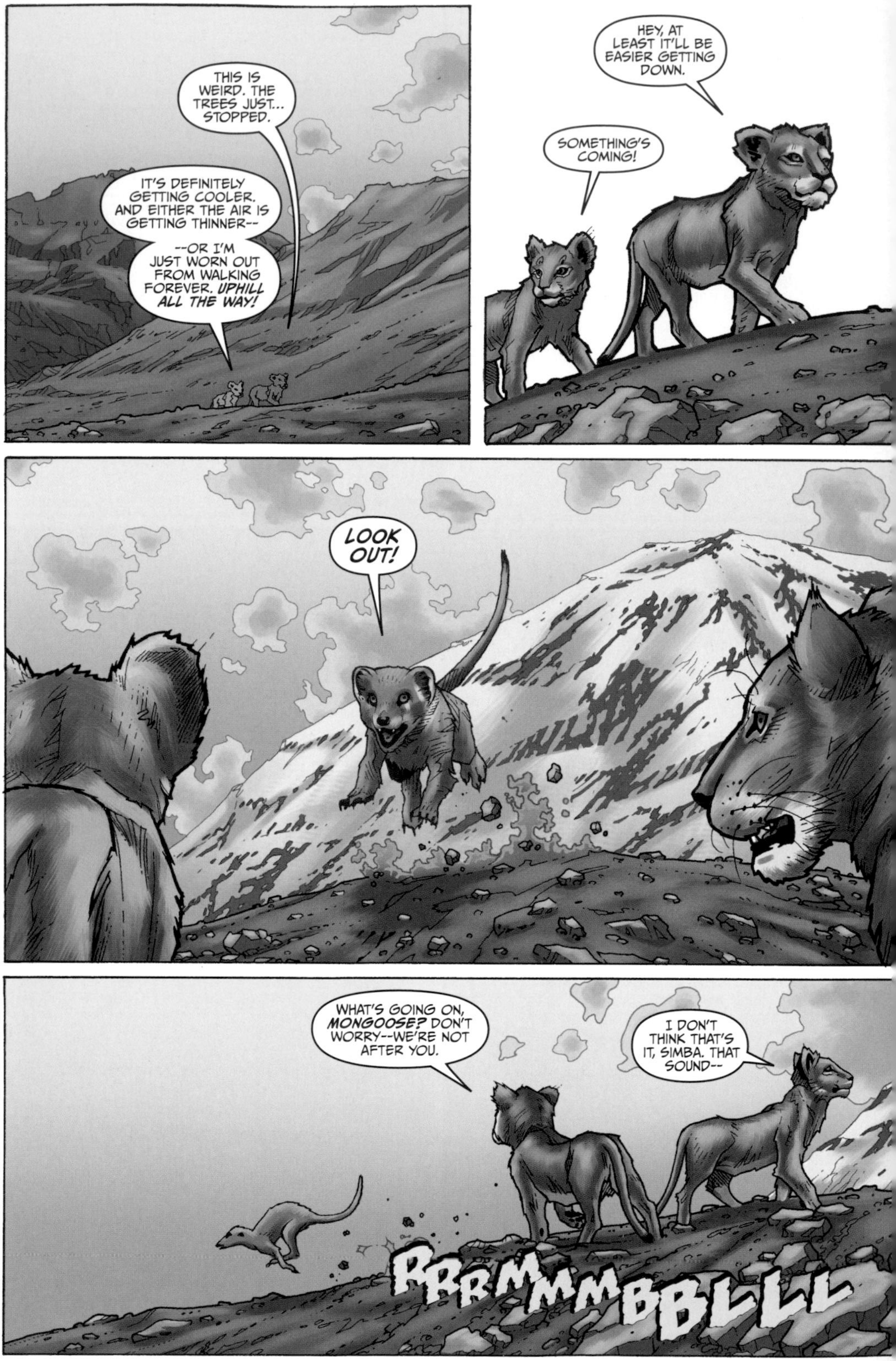
THIS IS WEIRD. THE TREES JUST... STOPPED.
IT'S DEFINITELY GETTING COOLER. AND EITHER THE AIR IS GETTING THINNER--
--OR I'M JUST WORN OUT FROM WALKING FOREVER. *UPHILL ALL THE WAY!*
HEY, AT LEAST IT'LL BE EASIER GETTING DOWN.
SOMETHING'S COMING!
LOOK OUT!
WHAT'S GOING ON, *MONGOOSE?* DON'T WORRY--WE'RE NOT AFTER YOU.
I DON'T THINK THAT'S IT, SIMBA. THAT SOUND--
RRRMMMBBLLL

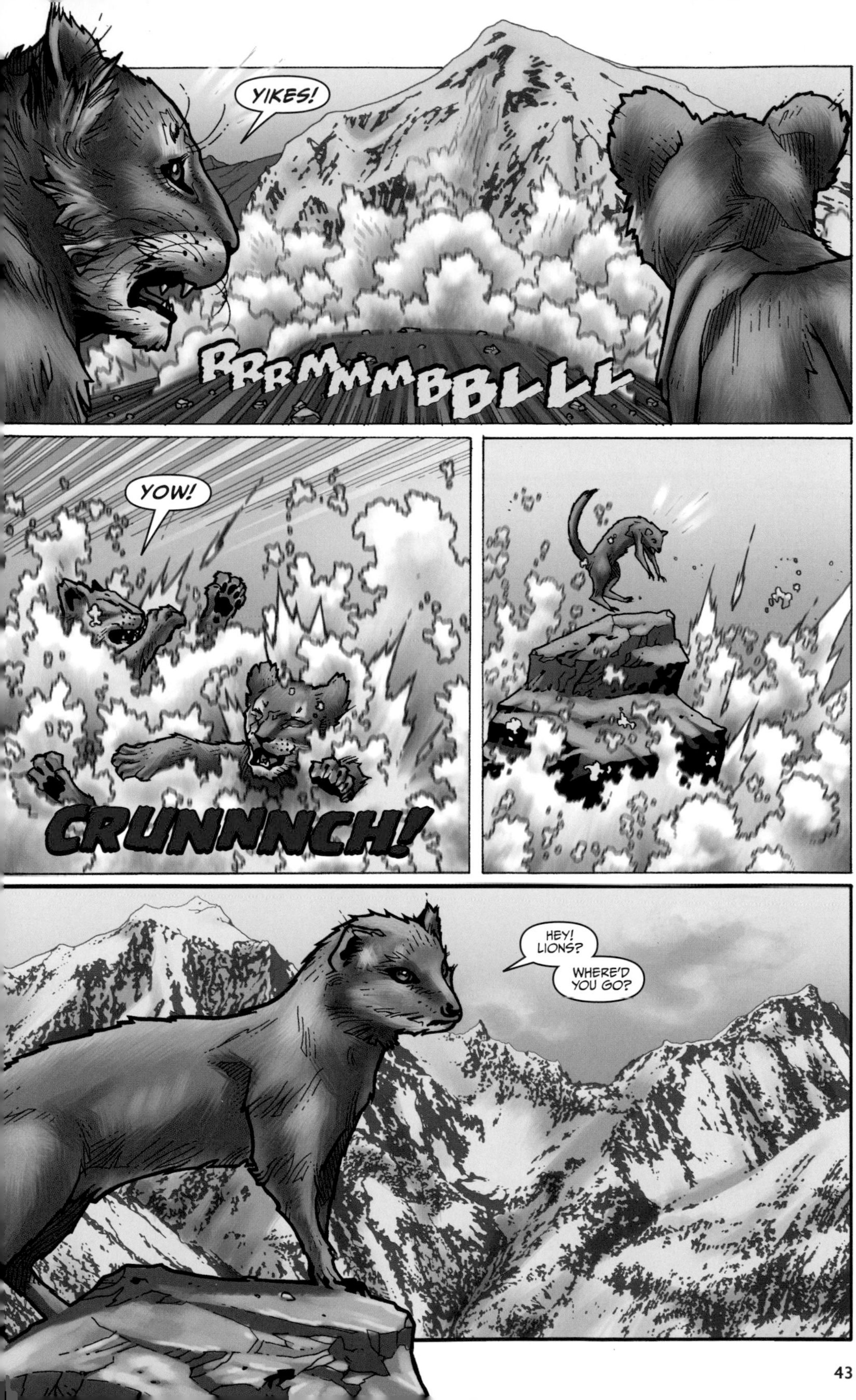
YIKES!
RRRMMMMBBLLL
YOW!
CRUNNNCH!
HEY! LIONS?
WHERE'D YOU GO?

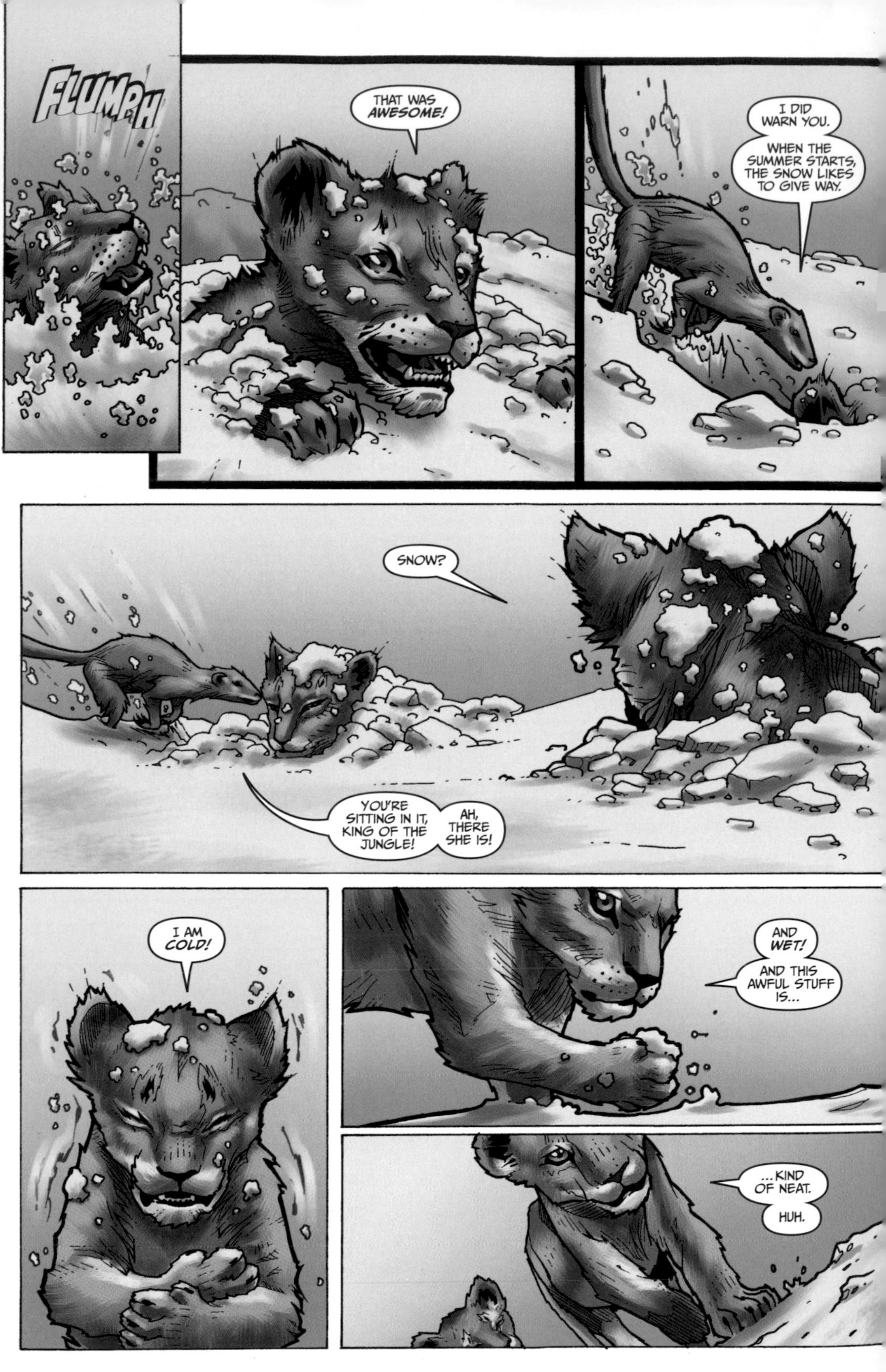
FLUMPH
THAT WAS AWESOME!
I DID WARN YOU.
WHEN THE SUMMER STARTS, THE SNOW LIKES TO GIVE WAY.
SNOW?
YOU'RE SITTING IN IT, KING OF THE JUNGLE!
AH, THERE SHE IS!
I AM COLD!
AND WET!
AND THIS AWFUL STUFF IS...
...KIND OF NEAT.
HUH.

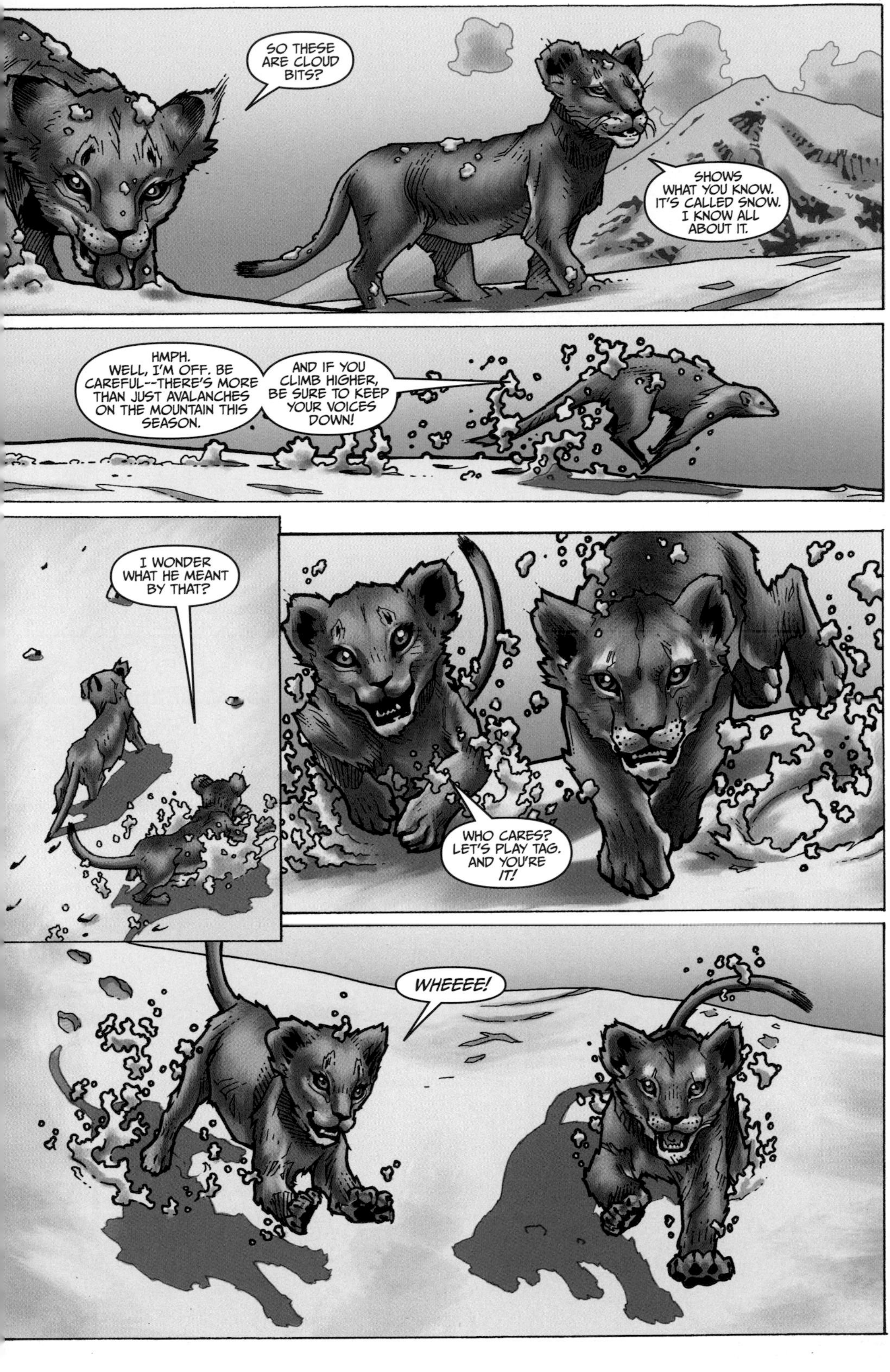
SO THESE ARE CLOUD BITS?
SHOWS WHAT YOU KNOW. IT'S CALLED SNOW. I KNOW ALL ABOUT IT.
HMPH. WELL, I'M OFF. BE CAREFUL--THERE'S MORE THAN JUST AVALANCHES ON THE MOUNTAIN THIS SEASON.
AND IF YOU CLIMB HIGHER, BE SURE TO KEEP YOUR VOICES DOWN!
I WONDER WHAT HE MEANT BY THAT?
WHO CARES? LET'S PLAY TAG. AND YOU'RE IT!
WHEEEE!

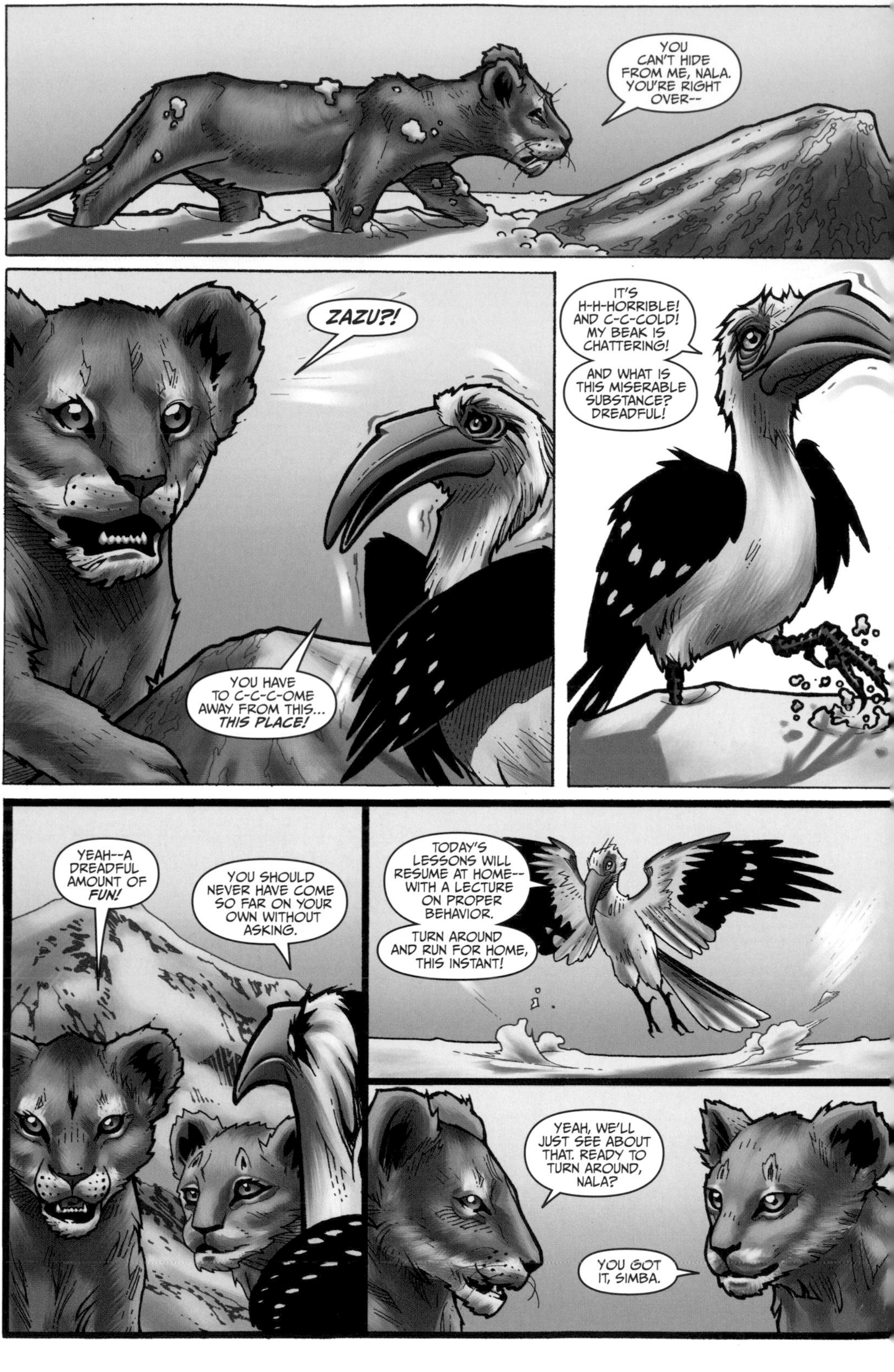
YOU CAN'T HIDE FROM ME, NALA. YOU'RE RIGHT OVER--
ZAZU?!
YOU HAVE TO C-C-C-OME AWAY FROM THIS... THIS PLACE!
IT'S H-H-HORRIBLE! AND C-C-COLD! MY BEAK IS CHATTERING!
AND WHAT IS THIS MISERABLE SUBSTANCE? DREADFUL!
YEAH--A DREADFUL AMOUNT OF FUN!
YOU SHOULD NEVER HAVE COME SO FAR ON YOUR OWN WITHOUT ASKING.
TODAY'S LESSONS WILL RESUME AT HOME--WITH A LECTURE ON PROPER BEHAVIOR.
TURN AROUND AND RUN FOR HOME, THIS INSTANT!
YEAH, WE'LL JUST SEE ABOUT THAT. READY TO TURN AROUND, NALA?
YOU GOT IT, SIMBA.

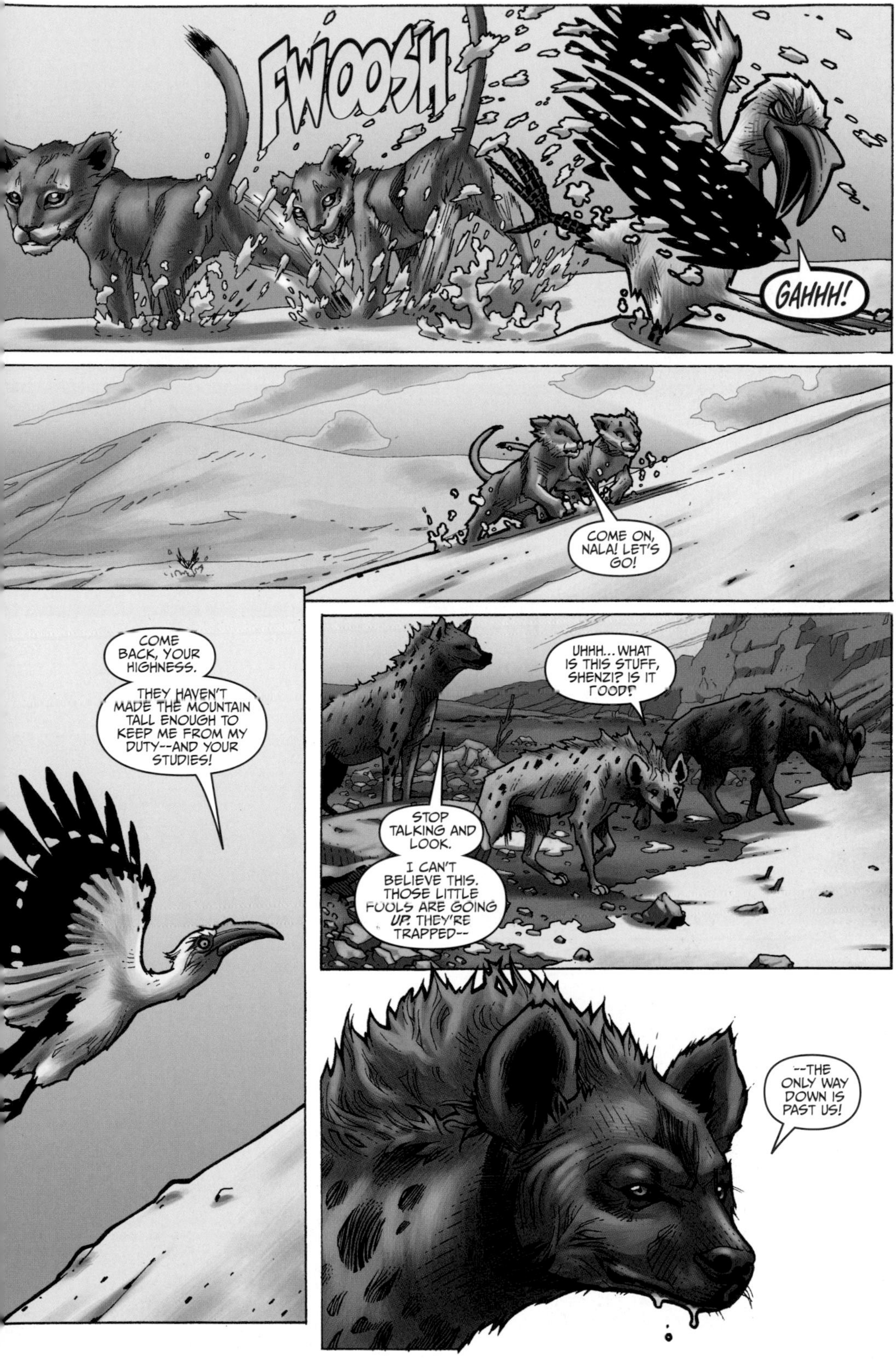
FWOOSH
GAHHH!
COME ON, NALA! LET'S GO!
COME BACK, YOUR HIGHNESS.
THEY HAVEN'T MADE THE MOUNTAIN TALL ENOUGH TO KEEP ME FROM MY DUTY--AND YOUR STUDIES!
UHHH... WHAT IS THIS STUFF, SHENZI? IS IT FOOD?
STOP TALKING AND LOOK.
I CAN'T BELIEVE THIS. THOSE LITTLE FOOLS ARE GOING UP. THEY'RE TRAPPED--
--THE ONLY WAY DOWN IS PAST US!

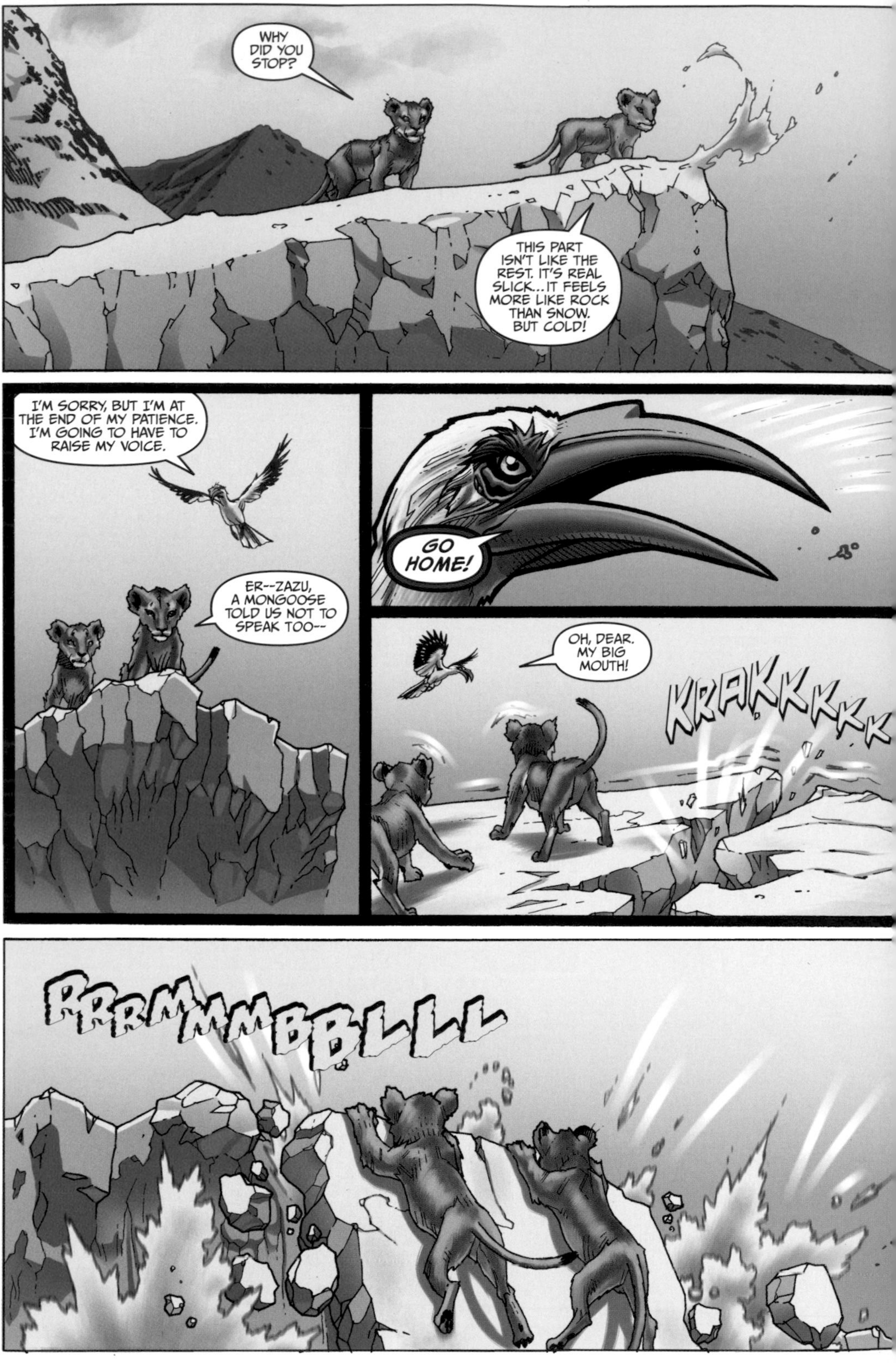
WHY DID YOU STOP?
THIS PART ISN'T LIKE THE REST. IT'S REAL SLICK...IT FEELS MORE LIKE ROCK THAN SNOW. BUT COLD!
I'M SORRY, BUT I'M AT THE END OF MY PATIENCE. I'M GOING TO HAVE TO RAISE MY VOICE.
ER--ZAZU, A MONGOOSE TOLD US NOT TO SPEAK TOO--
GO HOME!
OH, DEAR. MY BIG MOUTH!
KRAKKKKK
RRRMMMBBLLL

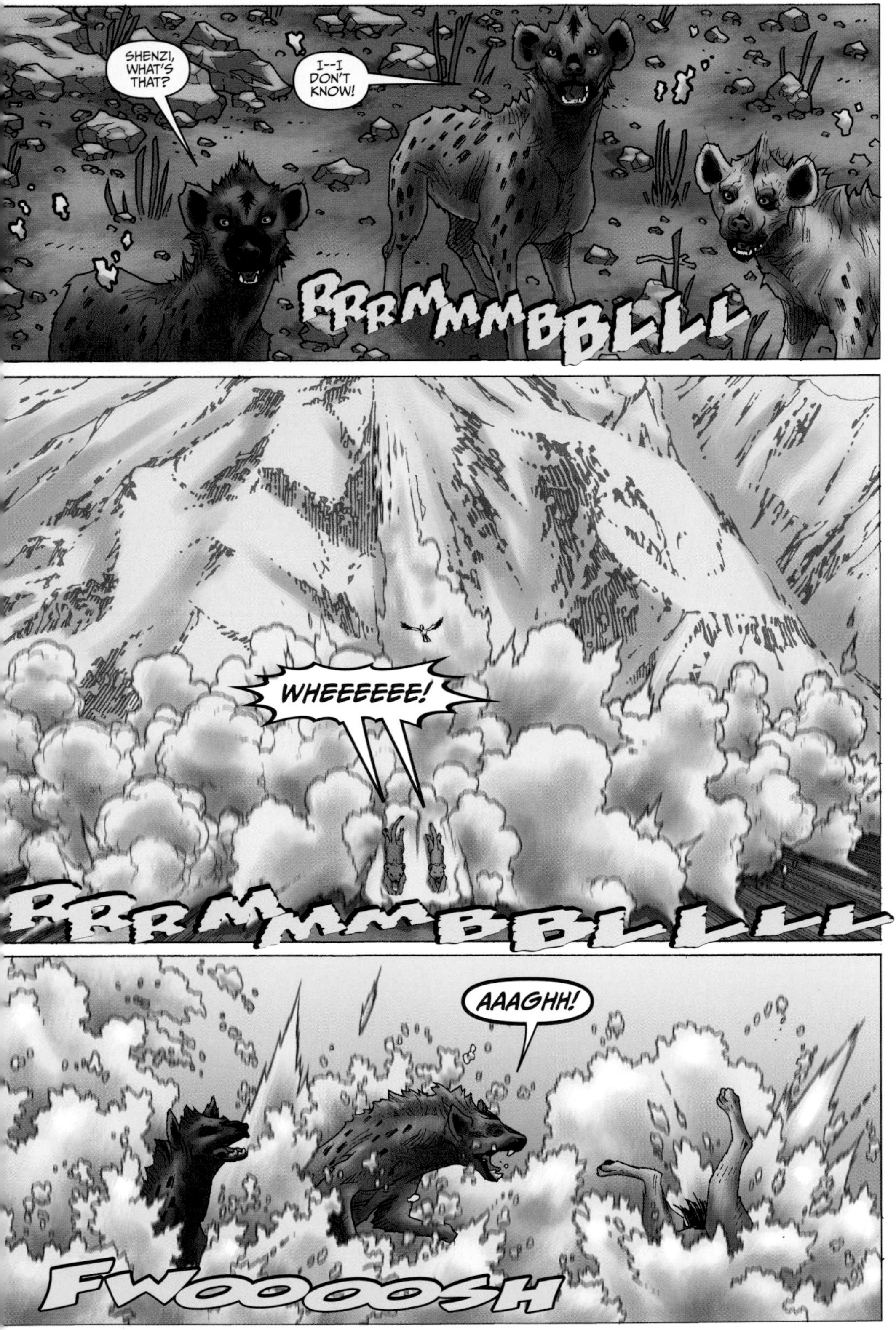
SHENZI, WHAT'S THAT?
I--I DON'T KNOW!
RRRMMMBBLLL
WHEEEEEE!
RRRMMMBBLLLL
AAAGHH!
FWOOOOSH

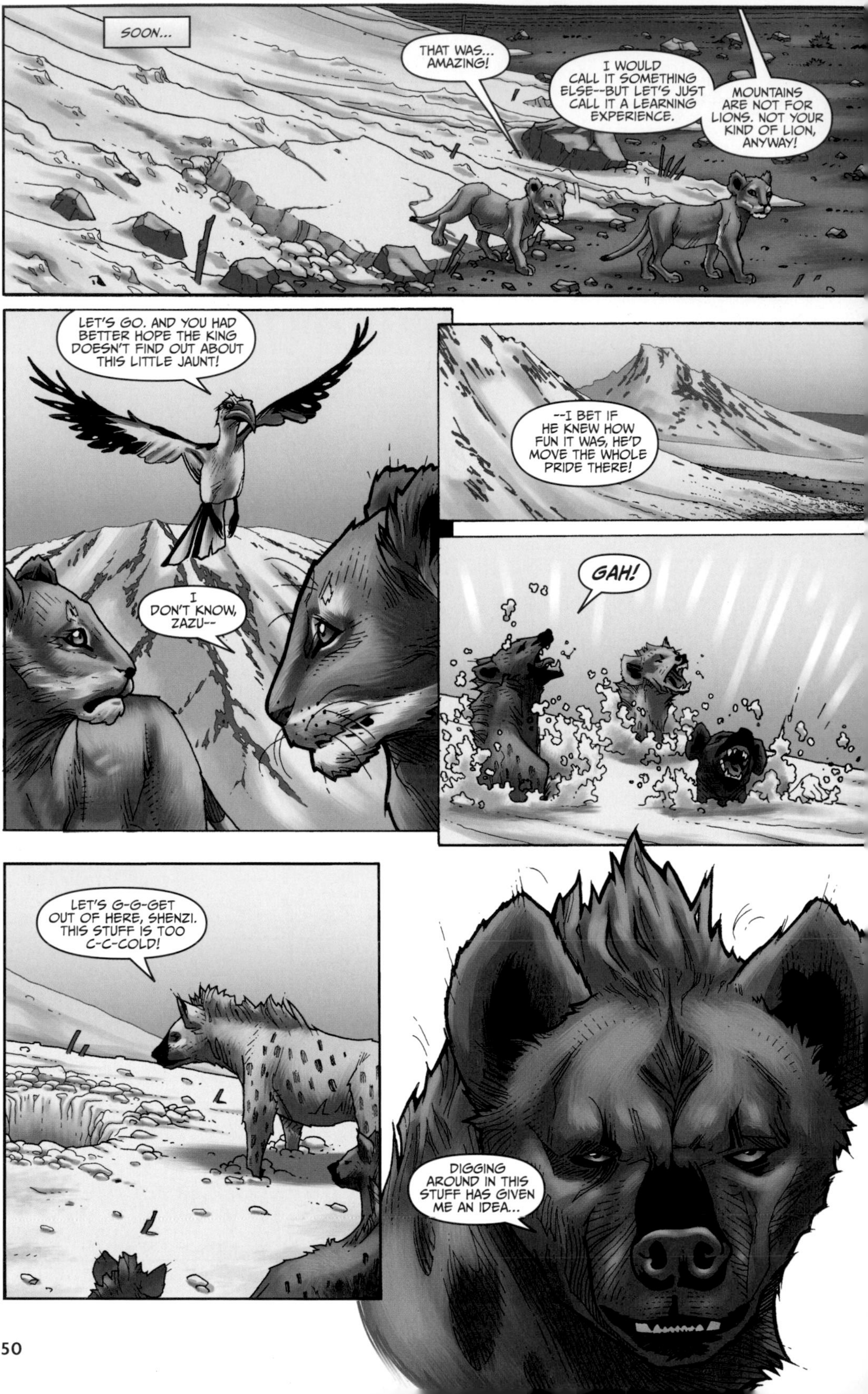
SOON...
THAT WAS... AMAZING!
I WOULD CALL IT SOMETHING ELSE--BUT LET'S JUST CALL IT A LEARNING EXPERIENCE.
MOUNTAINS ARE NOT FOR LIONS. NOT YOUR KIND OF LION, ANYWAY!
LET'S GO. AND YOU HAD BETTER HOPE THE KING DOESN'T FIND OUT ABOUT THIS LITTLE JAUNT!
I DON'T KNOW, ZAZU--
--I BET IF HE KNEW HOW FUN IT WAS, HE'D MOVE THE WHOLE PRIDE THERE!
GAH!
LET'S G-G-GET OUT OF HERE, SHENZI. THIS STUFF IS TOO C-C-COLD!
DIGGING AROUND IN THIS STUFF HAS GIVEN ME AN IDEA...

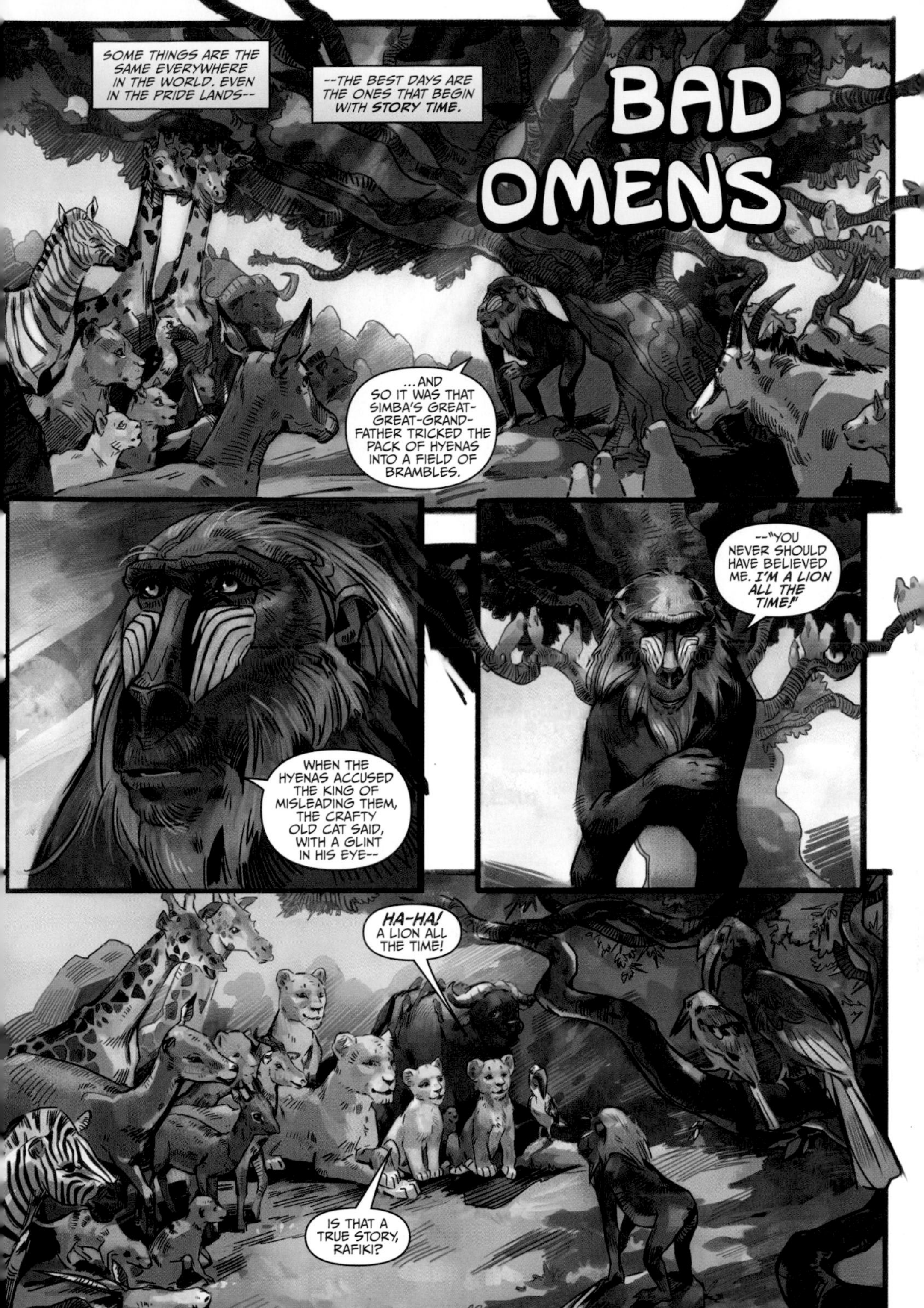
SOME THINGS ARE THE SAME EVERYWHERE IN THE WORLD. EVEN IN THE PRIDE LANDS--
--THE BEST DAYS ARE THE ONES THAT BEGIN WITH STORY TIME.
BAD OMENS
...AND SO IT WAS THAT SIMBA'S GREAT-GREAT-GRAND-FATHER TRICKED THE PACK OF HYENAS INTO A FIELD OF BRAMBLES.
WHEN THE HYENAS ACCUSED THE KING OF MISLEADING THEM, THE CRAFTY OLD CAT SAID, WITH A GLINT IN HIS EYE--
--"YOU NEVER SHOULD HAVE BELIEVED ME. I'M A LION ALL THE TIME!"
HA-HA! A LION ALL THE TIME!
IS THAT A TRUE STORY, RAFIKI?

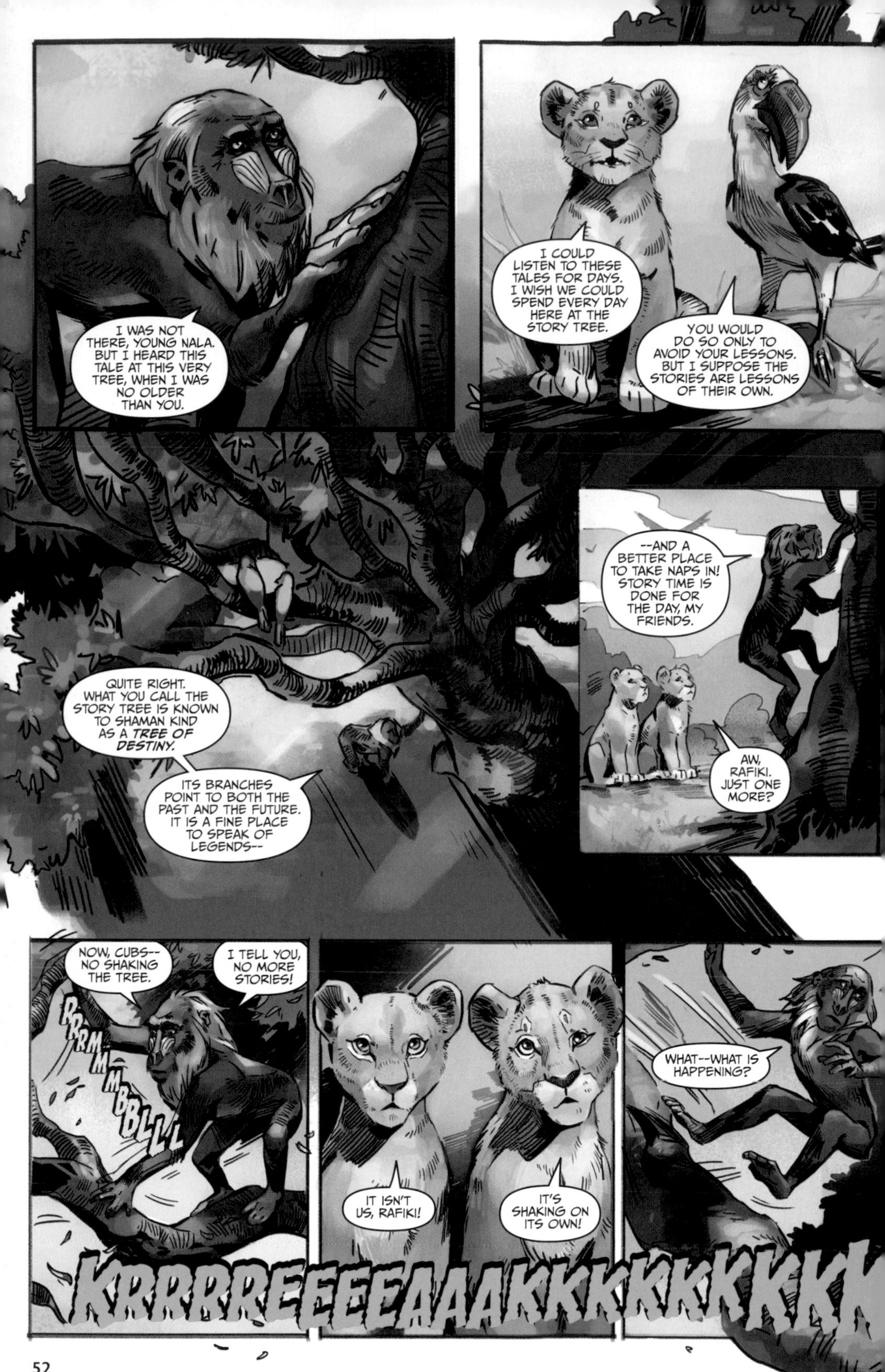

I WAS NOT THERE, YOUNG NALA. BUT I HEARD THIS TALE AT THIS VERY TREE, WHEN I WAS NO OLDER THAN YOU.
I COULD LISTEN TO THESE TALES FOR DAYS. I WISH WE COULD SPEND EVERY DAY HERE AT THE STORY TREE.
YOU WOULD DO SO ONLY TO AVOID YOUR LESSONS. BUT I SUPPOSE THE STORIES ARE LESSONS OF THEIR OWN.
QUITE RIGHT. WHAT YOU CALL THE STORY TREE IS KNOWN TO SHAMAN KIND AS A *TREE OF DESTINY.*
ITS BRANCHES POINT TO BOTH THE PAST AND THE FUTURE. IT IS A FINE PLACE TO SPEAK OF LEGENDS--
--AND A BETTER PLACE TO TAKE NAPS IN! STORY TIME IS DONE FOR THE DAY, MY FRIENDS.
AW, RAFIKI. JUST ONE MORE?
NOW, CUBS-- NO SHAKING THE TREE.
I TELL YOU, NO MORE STORIES!
RRRMMMBBLLL
IT ISN'T US, RAFIKI!
IT'S SHAKING ON ITS OWN!
WHAT--WHAT IS HAPPENING?
KRRRREEEEAAAKKKKKKKKK

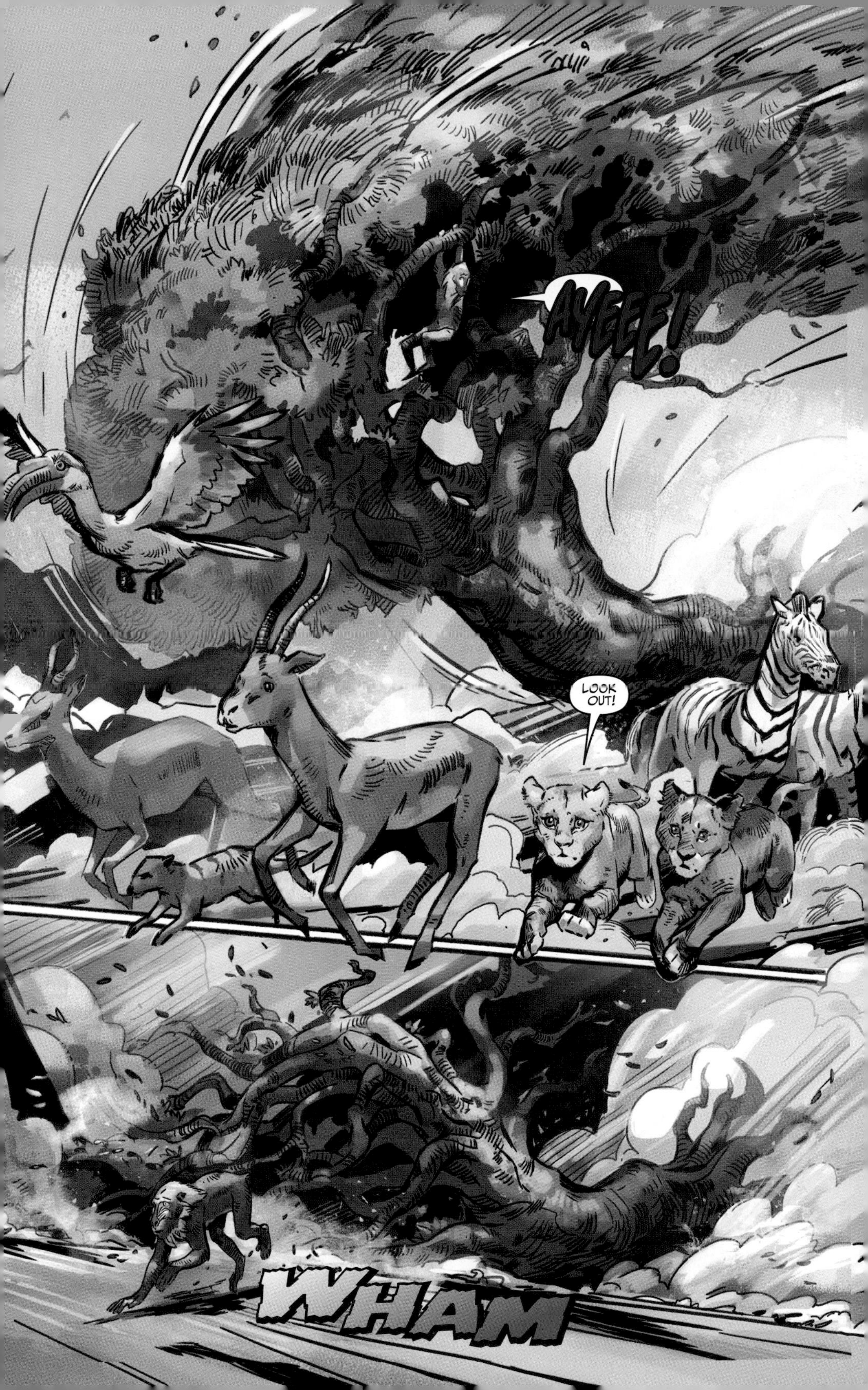
AYEEE!
LOOK OUT!
WHAM

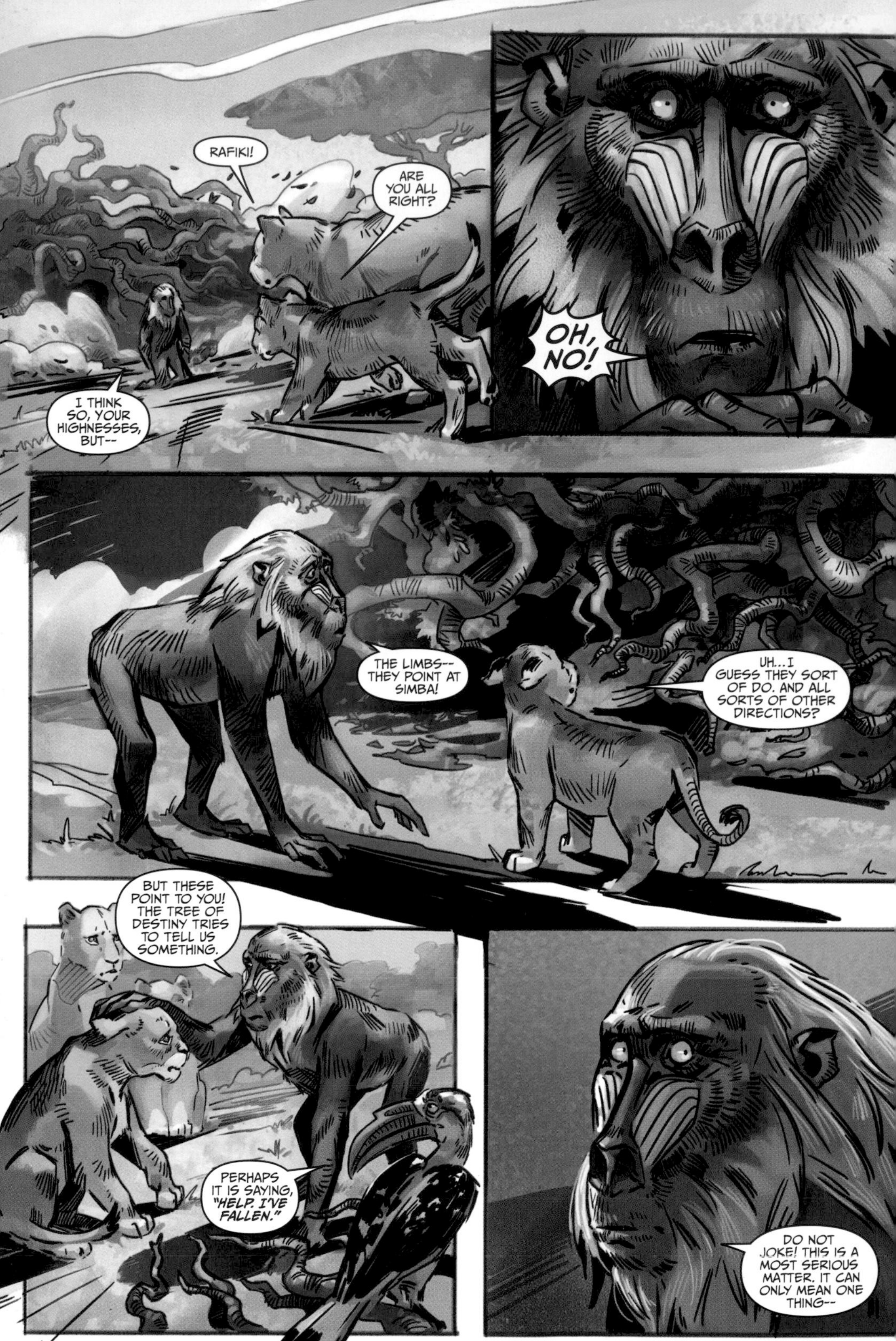
RAFIKI!
ARE YOU ALL RIGHT?
I THINK SO, YOUR HIGHNESSES, BUT--
OH, NO!
THE LIMBS-- THEY POINT AT SIMBA!
UH...I GUESS THEY SORT OF DO. AND ALL SORTS OF OTHER DIRECTIONS?
BUT THESE POINT TO YOU! THE TREE OF DESTINY TRIES TO TELL US SOMETHING.
PERHAPS IT IS SAYING, *"HELP. I'VE FALLEN."*
DO NOT JOKE! THIS IS A MOST SERIOUS MATTER. IT CAN ONLY MEAN ONE THING--

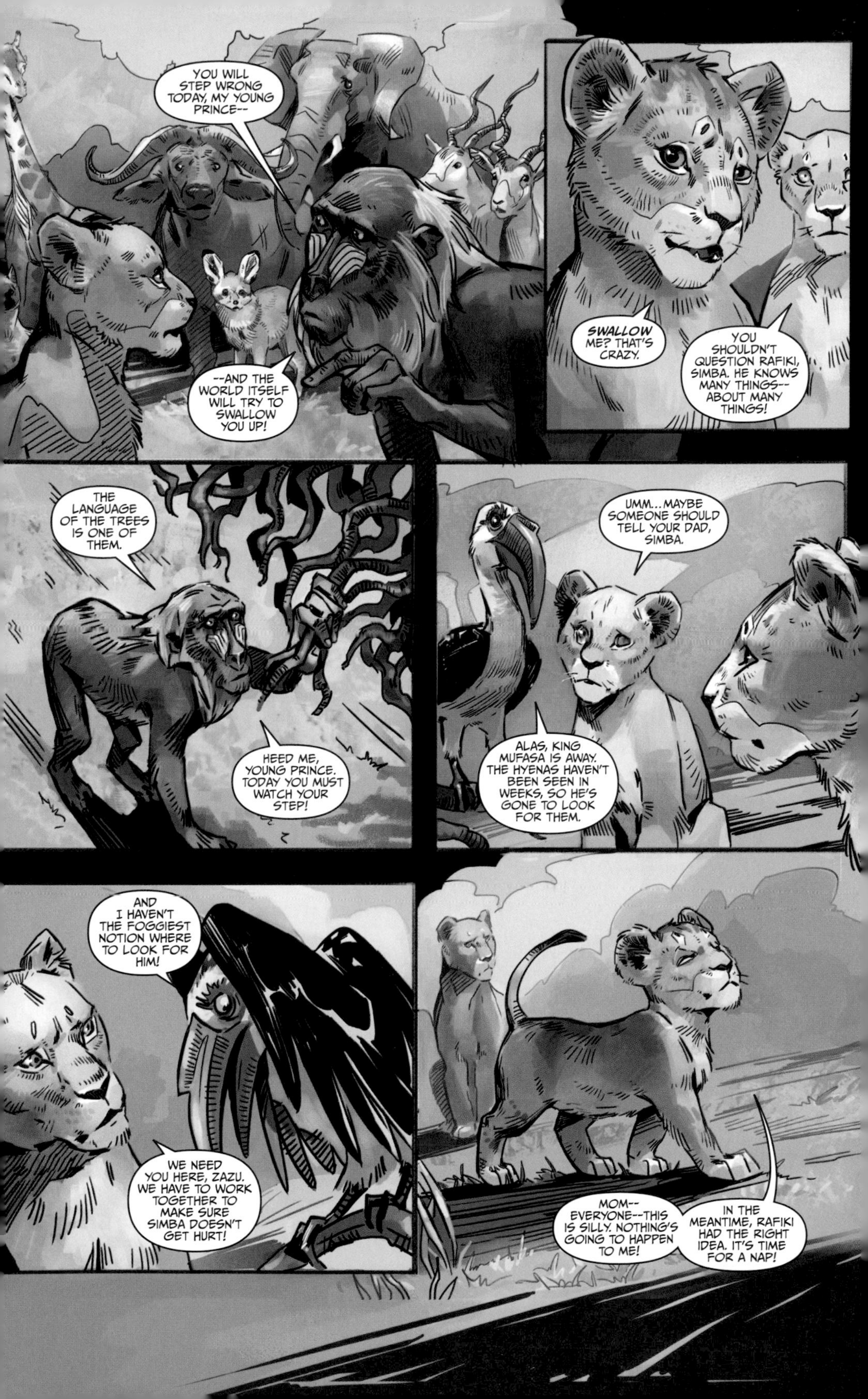
YOU WILL STEP WRONG TODAY, MY YOUNG PRINCE--
--AND THE WORLD ITSELF WILL TRY TO SWALLOW YOU UP!
SWALLOW ME? THAT'S CRAZY.
YOU SHOULDN'T QUESTION RAFIKI, SIMBA. HE KNOWS MANY THINGS-- ABOUT MANY THINGS!
THE LANGUAGE OF THE TREES IS ONE OF THEM.
HEED ME, YOUNG PRINCE. TODAY YOU MUST WATCH YOUR STEP!
UMM... MAYBE SOMEONE SHOULD TELL YOUR DAD, SIMBA.
ALAS, KING MUFASA IS AWAY. THE HYENAS HAVEN'T BEEN SEEN IN WEEKS, SO HE'S GONE TO LOOK FOR THEM.
AND I HAVEN'T THE FOGGIEST NOTION WHERE TO LOOK FOR HIM!
WE NEED YOU HERE, ZAZU. WE HAVE TO WORK TOGETHER TO MAKE SURE SIMBA DOESN'T GET HURT!
MOM-- EVERYONE--THIS IS SILLY. NOTHING'S GOING TO HAPPEN TO ME!
IN THE MEANTIME, RAFIKI HAD THE RIGHT IDEA. IT'S TIME FOR A NAP!

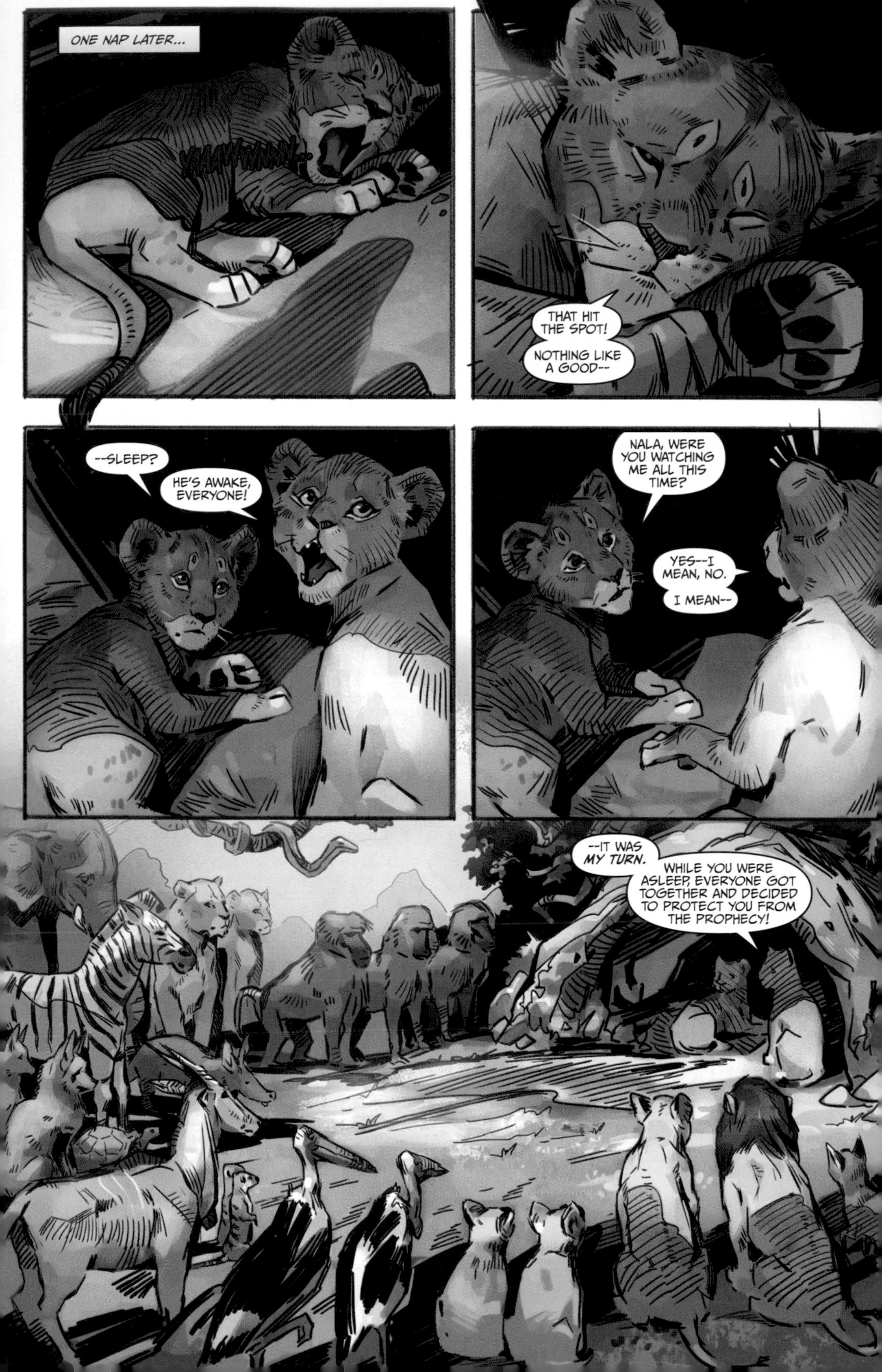
ONE NAP LATER...
THAT HIT THE SPOT!
NOTHING LIKE A GOOD--
--SLEEP?
HE'S AWAKE, EVERYONE!
NALA, WERE YOU WATCHING ME ALL THIS TIME?
YES--I MEAN, NO.
I MEAN--
--IT WAS *MY TURN.*
WHILE YOU WERE ASLEEP, EVERYONE GOT TOGETHER AND DECIDED TO PROTECT YOU FROM THE PROPHECY!

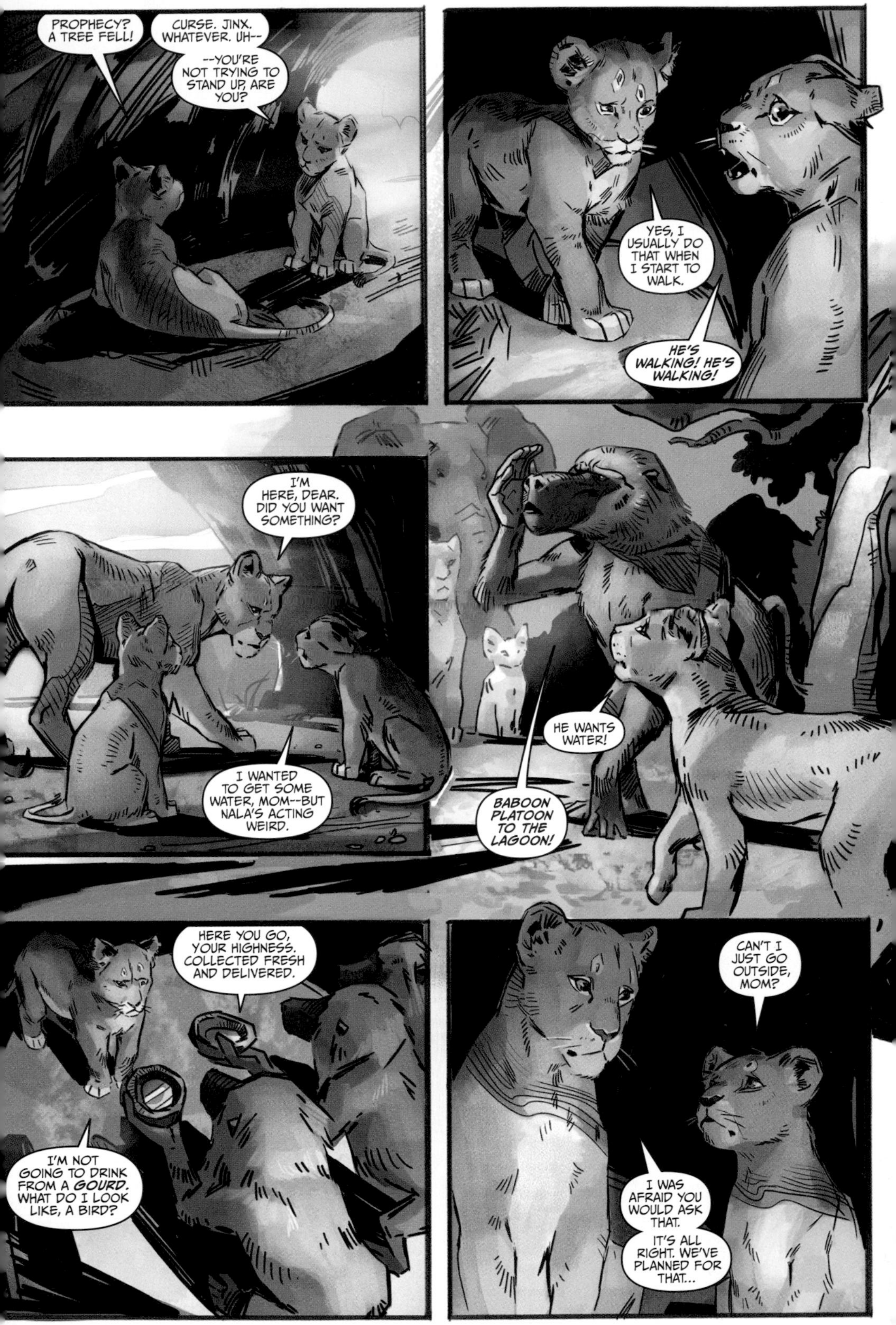
PROPHECY? A TREE FELL!
CURSE. JINX. WHATEVER. UH--
--YOU'RE NOT TRYING TO STAND UP, ARE YOU?
YES, I USUALLY DO THAT WHEN I START TO WALK.
HE'S WALKING! HE'S WALKING!
I'M HERE, DEAR. DID YOU WANT SOMETHING?
I WANTED TO GET SOME WATER, MOM--BUT NALA'S ACTING WEIRD.
HE WANTS WATER!
BABOON PLATOON TO THE LAGOON!
HERE YOU GO, YOUR HIGHNESS. COLLECTED FRESH AND DELIVERED.
I'M NOT GOING TO DRINK FROM A GOURD. WHAT DO I LOOK LIKE, A BIRD?
CAN'T I JUST GO OUTSIDE, MOM?
I WAS AFRAID YOU WOULD ASK THAT.
IT'S ALL RIGHT. WE'VE PLANNED FOR THAT...

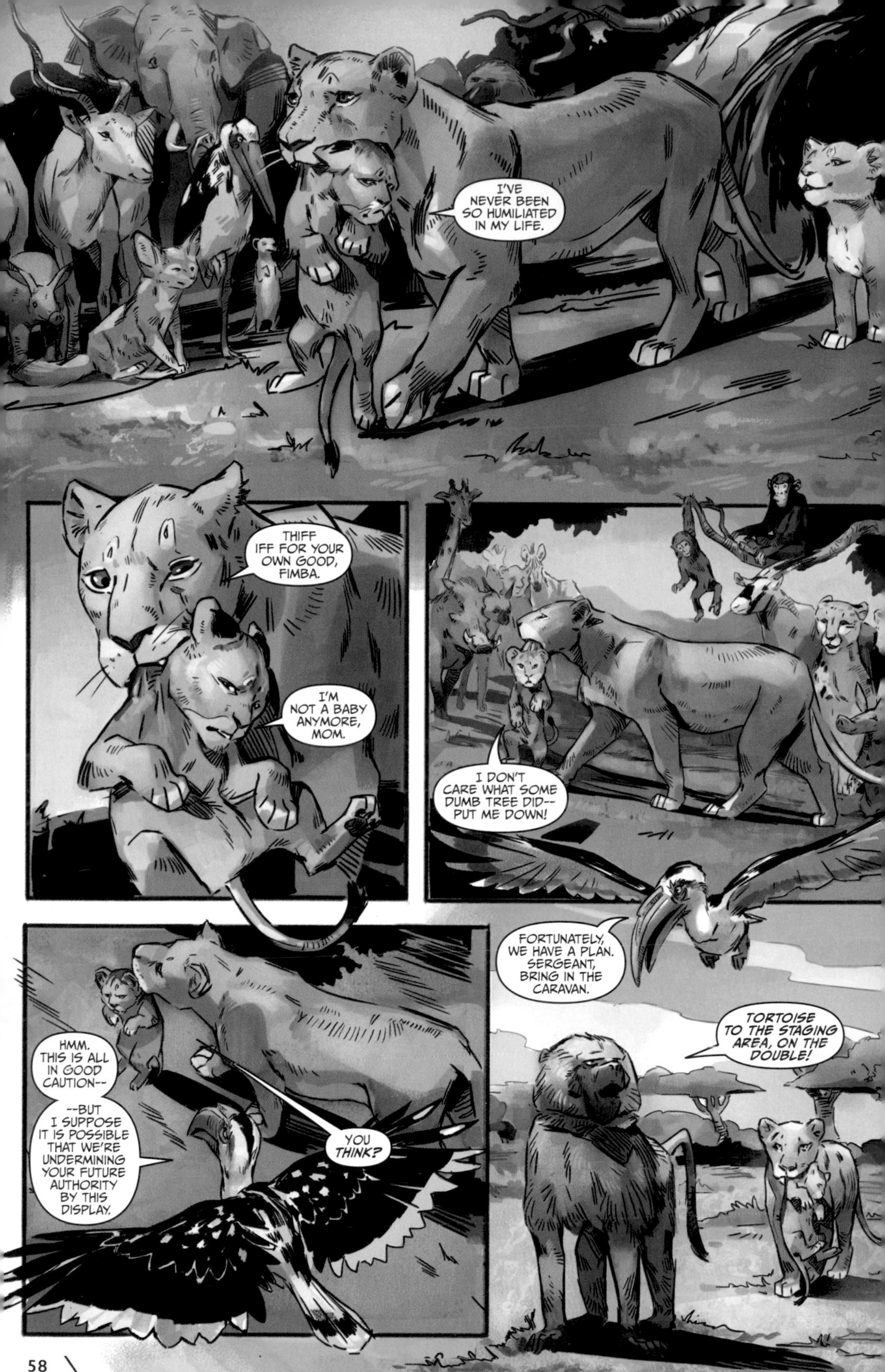
I'VE NEVER BEEN SO HUMILIATED IN MY LIFE.
THIFF IFF FOR YOUR OWN GOOD, FIMBA.
I'M NOT A BABY ANYMORE, MOM.
I DON'T CARE WHAT SOME DUMB TREE DID-- PUT ME DOWN!
HMM. THIS IS ALL IN GOOD CAUTION--
--BUT I SUPPOSE IT IS POSSIBLE THAT WE'RE UNDERMINING YOUR FUTURE AUTHORITY BY THIS DISPLAY.
YOU *THINK?*
FORTUNATELY, WE HAVE A PLAN. SERGEANT, BRING IN THE CARAVAN.
TORTOISE TO THE STAGING AREA, ON THE DOUBLE!

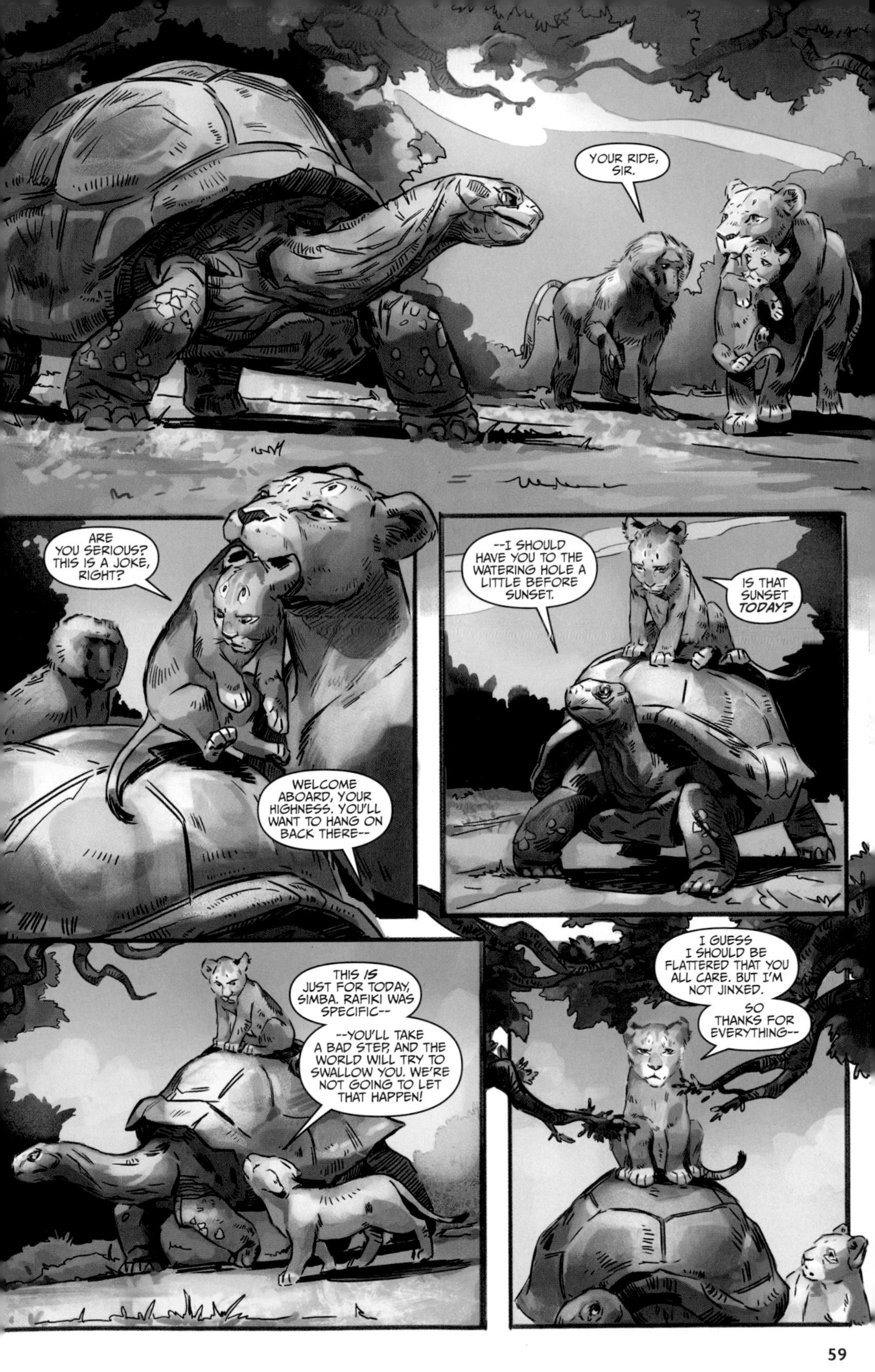
YOUR RIDE, SIR.
ARE YOU SERIOUS? THIS IS A JOKE, RIGHT?
WELCOME ABOARD, YOUR HIGHNESS. YOU'LL WANT TO HANG ON BACK THERE--
--I SHOULD HAVE YOU TO THE WATERING HOLE A LITTLE BEFORE SUNSET.
IS THAT SUNSET *TODAY?*
THIS *IS* JUST FOR TODAY, SIMBA. RAFIKI WAS SPECIFIC--
--YOU'LL TAKE A BAD STEP, AND THE WORLD WILL TRY TO SWALLOW YOU. WE'RE NOT GOING TO LET THAT HAPPEN!
I GUESS I SHOULD BE FLATTERED THAT YOU ALL CARE. BUT I'M NOT JINXED.
SO THANKS FOR EVERYTHING--

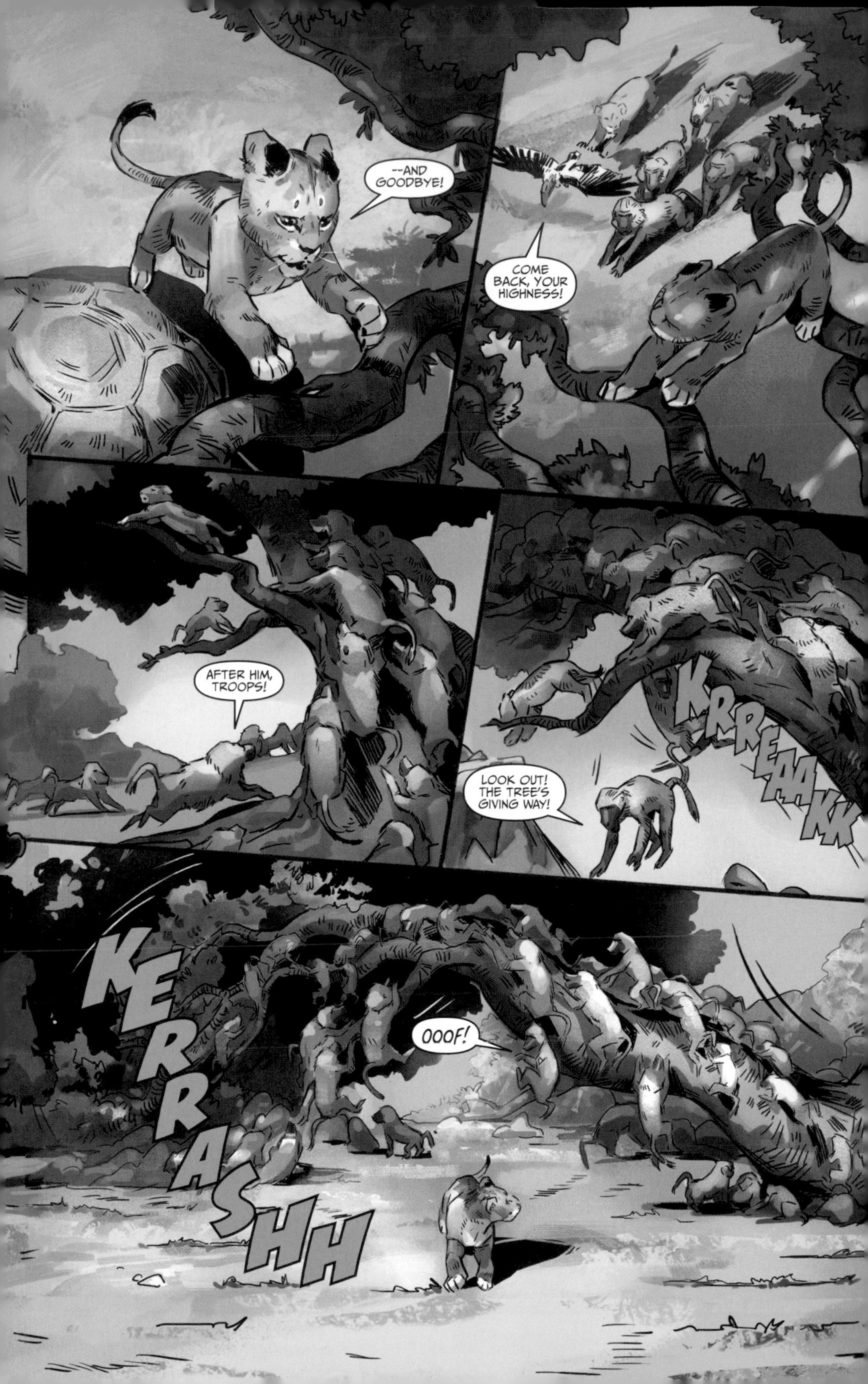
--AND GOODBYE!
COME BACK, YOUR HIGHNESS!
AFTER HIM, TROOPS!
KRREAAKK
LOOK OUT! THE TREE'S GIVING WAY!
KERRASHH
OOOF!

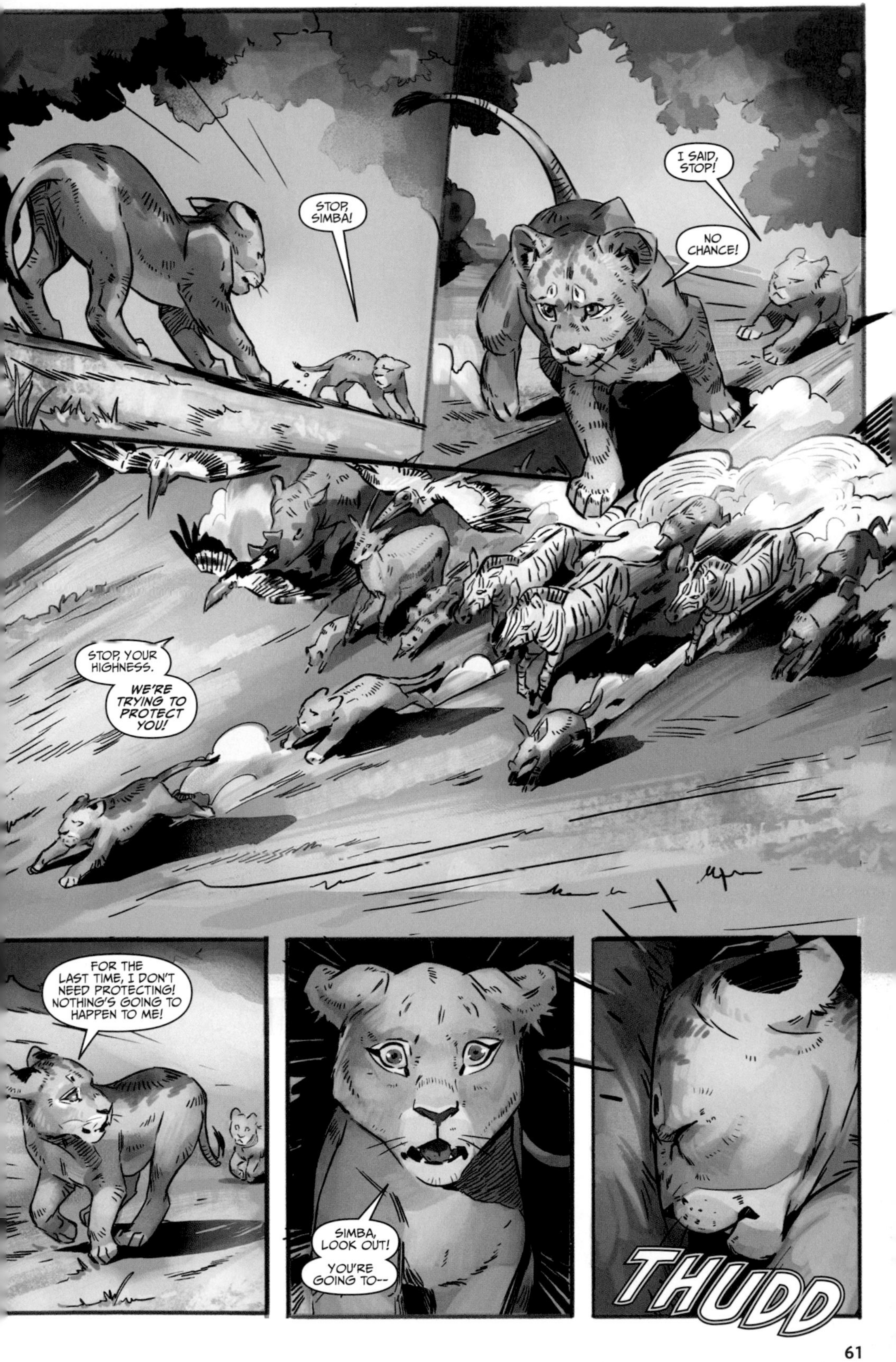
STOP, SIMBA!
I SAID, STOP!
NO CHANCE!
STOP, YOUR HIGHNESS.
WE'RE TRYING TO PROTECT YOU!
FOR THE LAST TIME, I DON'T NEED PROTECTING! NOTHING'S GOING TO HAPPEN TO ME!
SIMBA, LOOK OUT!
YOU'RE GOING TO--
THUDD

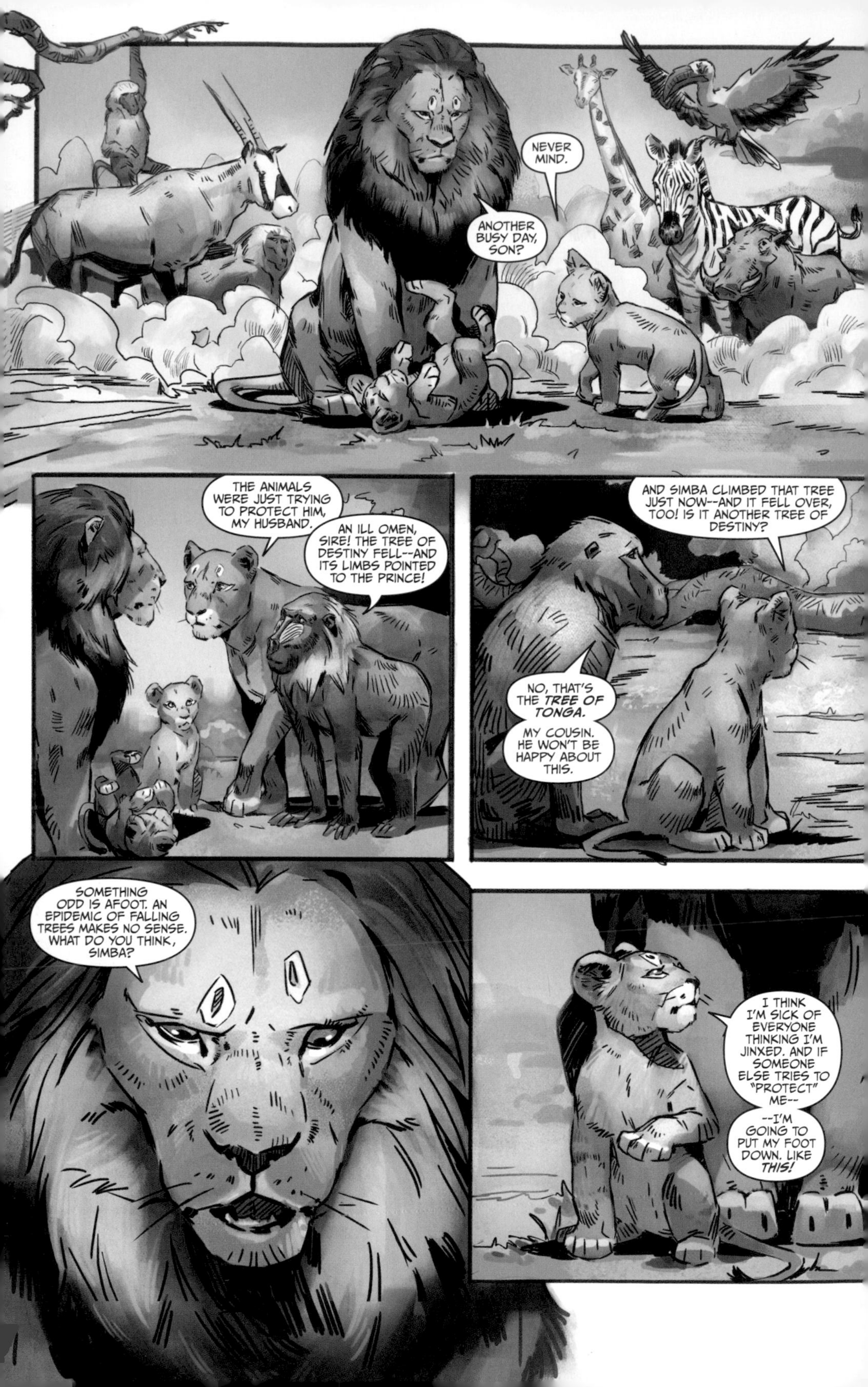

ANOTHER BUSY DAY, SON?
NEVER MIND.
THE ANIMALS WERE JUST TRYING TO PROTECT HIM, MY HUSBAND.
AN ILL OMEN, SIRE! THE TREE OF DESTINY FELL--AND ITS LIMBS POINTED TO THE PRINCE!
AND SIMBA CLIMBED THAT TREE JUST NOW--AND IT FELL OVER, TOO! IS IT ANOTHER TREE OF DESTINY?
NO, THAT'S THE ***TREE OF TONGA.***
MY COUSIN. HE WON'T BE HAPPY ABOUT THIS.
SOMETHING ODD IS AFOOT. AN EPIDEMIC OF FALLING TREES MAKES NO SENSE. WHAT DO YOU THINK, SIMBA?
I THINK I'M SICK OF EVERYONE THINKING I'M JINXED. AND IF SOMEONE ELSE TRIES TO "PROTECT" ME--
--I'M GOING TO PUT MY FOOT DOWN. LIKE ***THIS!***

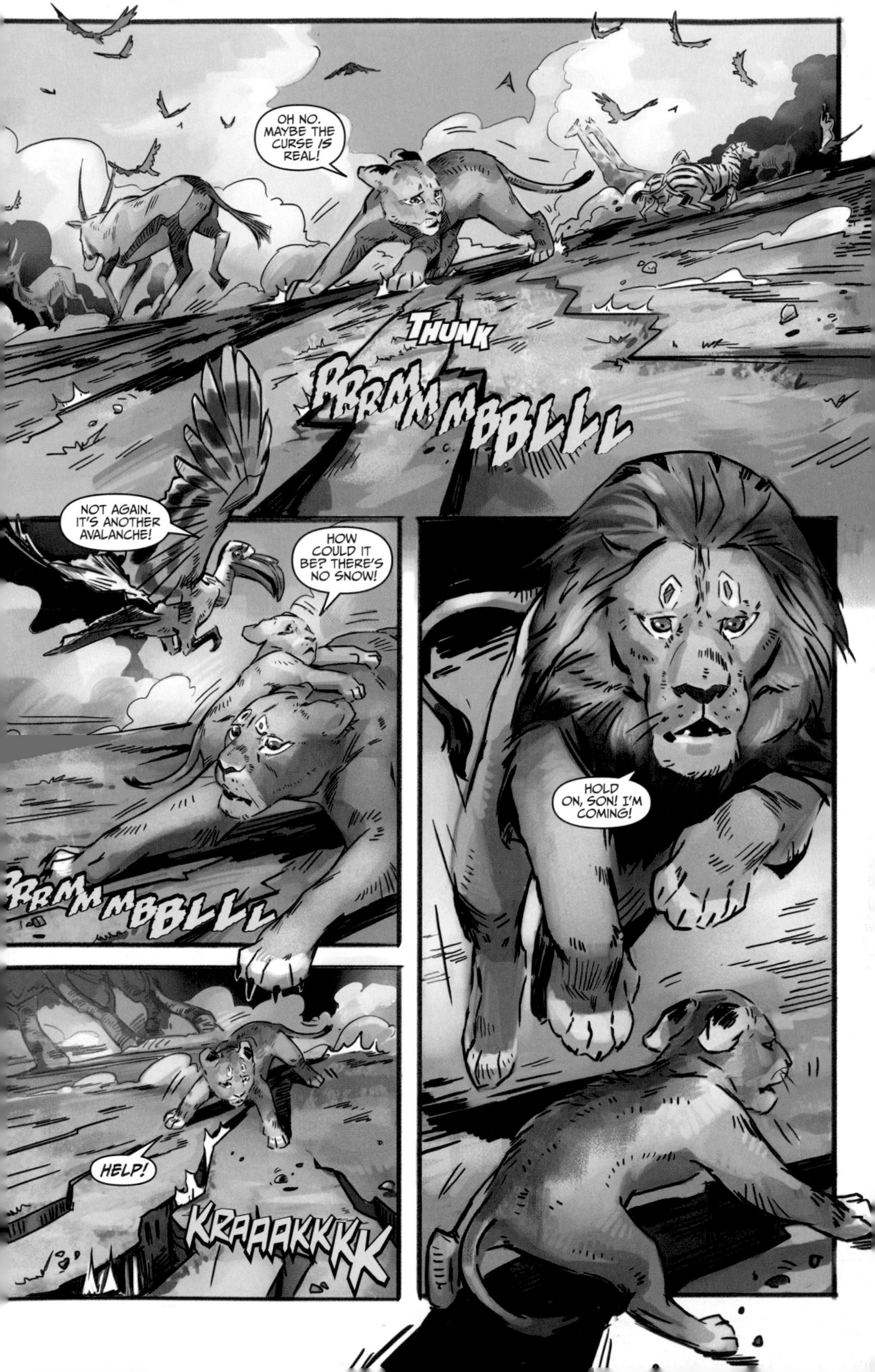
OH NO. MAYBE THE CURSE IS REAL!
THUNK
RRRMMMBBLLL
NOT AGAIN. IT'S ANOTHER AVALANCHE!
HOW COULD IT BE? THERE'S NO SNOW!
RRRMMMBBLLL
HOLD ON, SON! I'M COMING!
HELP!
KRAAAKKKK

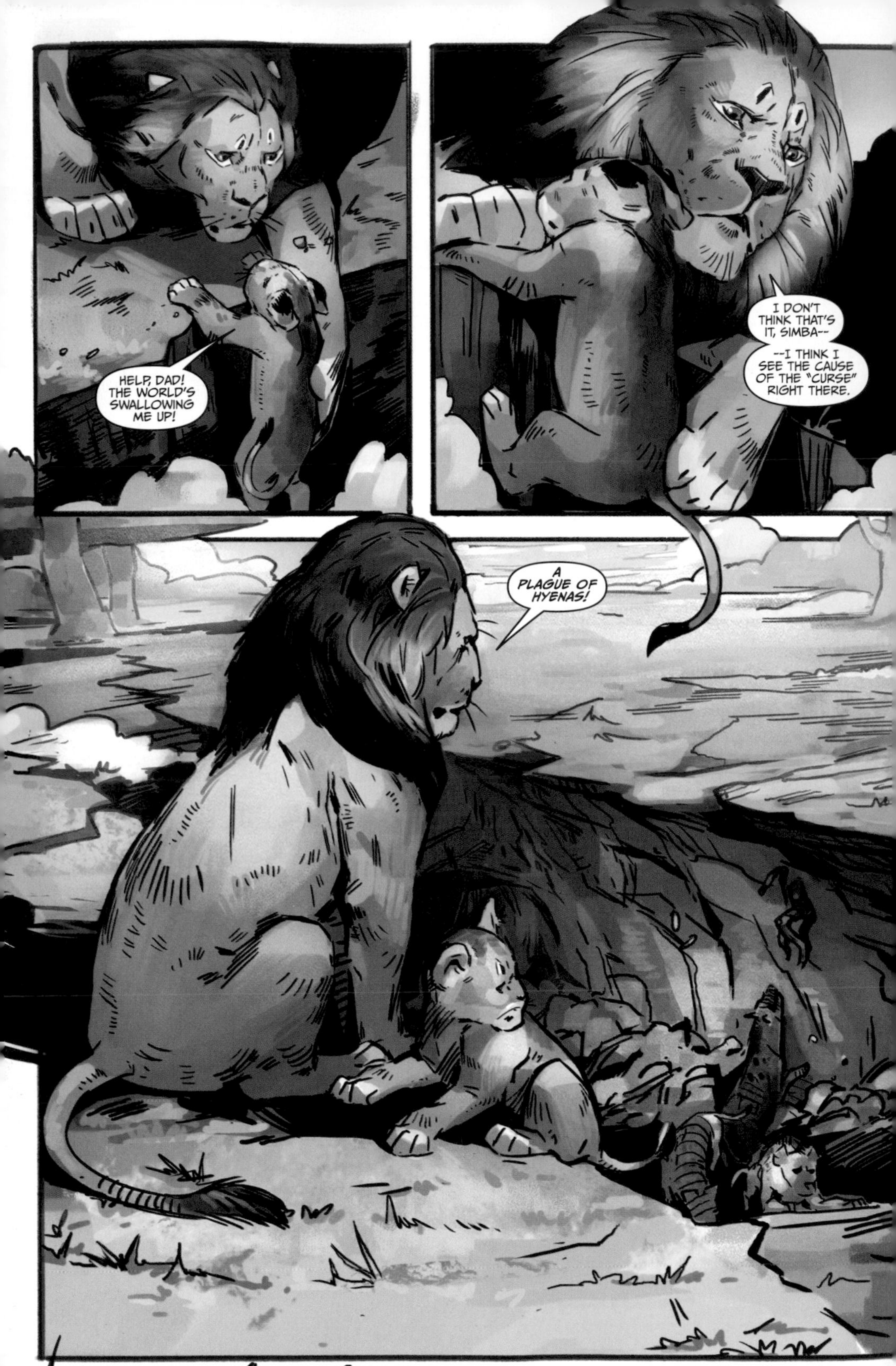
HELP, DAD! THE WORLD'S SWALLOWING ME UP!
I DON'T THINK THAT'S IT, SIMBA--
--I THINK I SEE THE CAUSE OF THE "CURSE" RIGHT THERE.
A PLAGUE OF HYENAS!

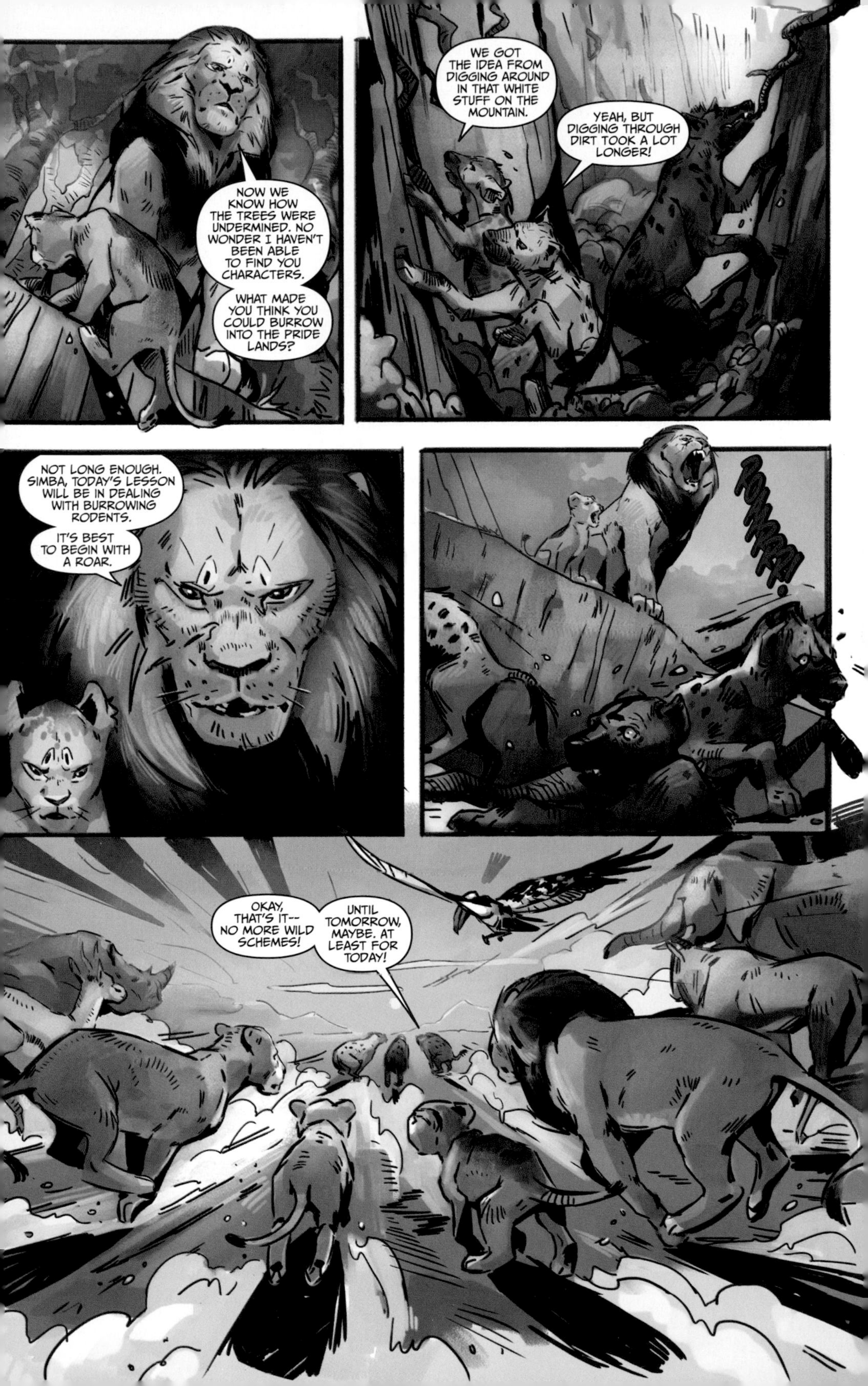
NOW WE KNOW HOW THE TREES WERE UNDERMINED. NO WONDER I HAVEN'T BEEN ABLE TO FIND YOU CHARACTERS.
WHAT MADE YOU THINK YOU COULD BURROW INTO THE PRIDE LANDS?
WE GOT THE IDEA FROM DIGGING AROUND IN THAT WHITE STUFF ON THE MOUNTAIN.
YEAH, BUT DIGGING THROUGH DIRT TOOK A LOT LONGER!
NOT LONG ENOUGH. SIMBA, TODAY'S LESSON WILL BE IN DEALING WITH BURROWING RODENTS.
IT'S BEST TO BEGIN WITH A ROAR.
OKAY, THAT'S IT-- NO MORE WILD SCHEMES!
UNTIL TOMORROW, MAYBE. AT LEAST FOR TODAY!

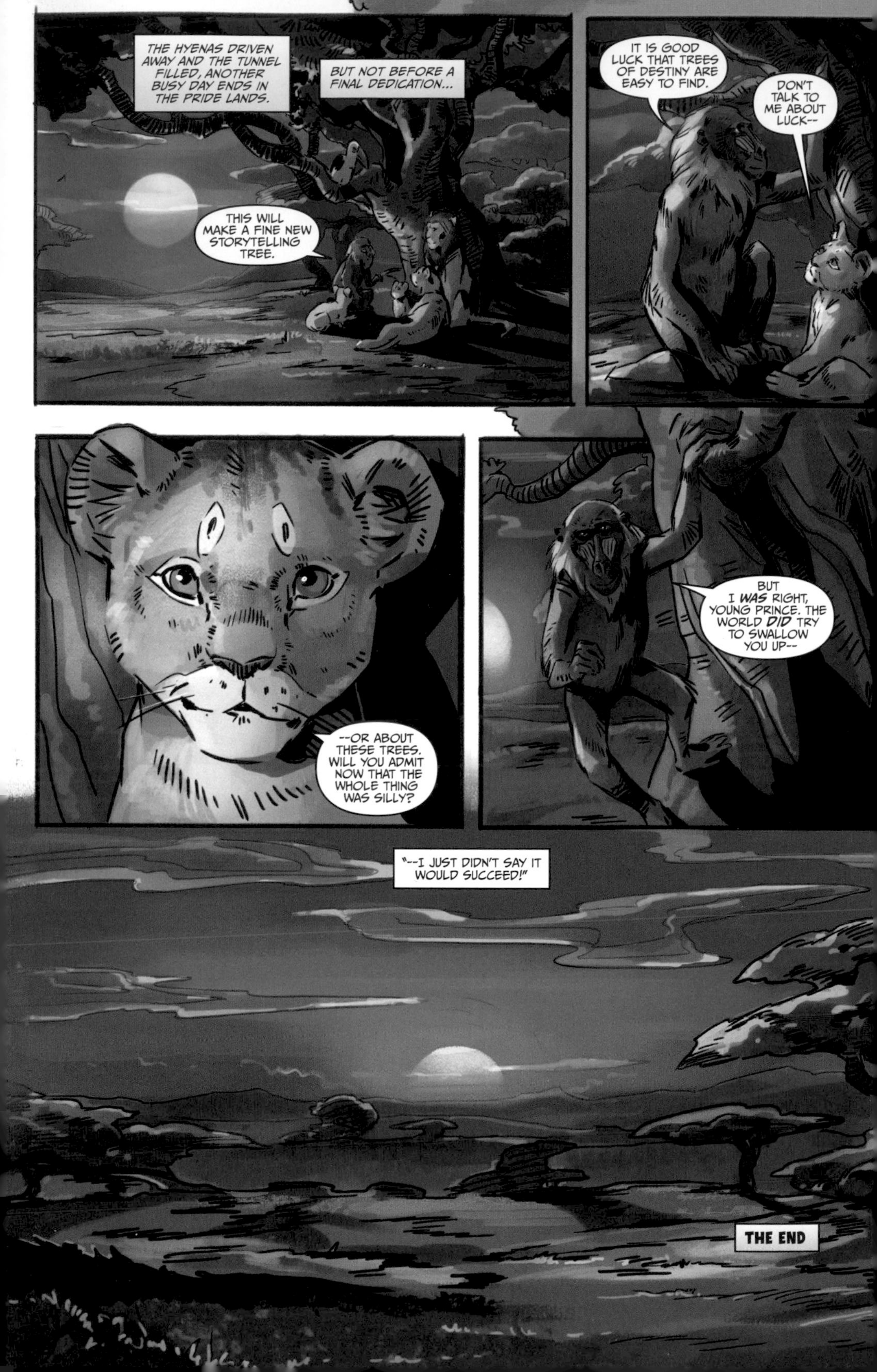
THE HYENAS DRIVEN AWAY AND THE TUNNEL FILLED, ANOTHER BUSY DAY ENDS IN THE PRIDE LANDS.
BUT NOT BEFORE A FINAL DEDICATION...
THIS WILL MAKE A FINE NEW STORYTELLING TREE.
IT IS GOOD LUCK THAT TREES OF DESTINY ARE EASY TO FIND.
DON'T TALK TO ME ABOUT LUCK--
--OR ABOUT THESE TREES. WILL YOU ADMIT NOW THAT THE WHOLE THING WAS SILLY?
BUT I WAS RIGHT, YOUNG PRINCE. THE WORLD DID TRY TO SWALLOW YOU UP--
"--I JUST DIDN'T SAY IT WOULD SUCCEED!"
THE END

THE LION KING

SKETCHBOOK

Disney's *The Lion King*, directed by Jon Favreau, journeys
to the African savanna where a future king is born.

As we began work for this film tie-in graphic novel, we
explored several art styles to bring these characters to
"life" on the page. All of the artists in our book were
challenged to keep the characters looking like animals,
to keep their movements true to reality.

On these pages you will see test drawings that were created
by artist Timothy Green II. He referenced the characters
from the feature and worked to maintain an accurate
depiction of animals in the wild.

Character sketch of young Simba.

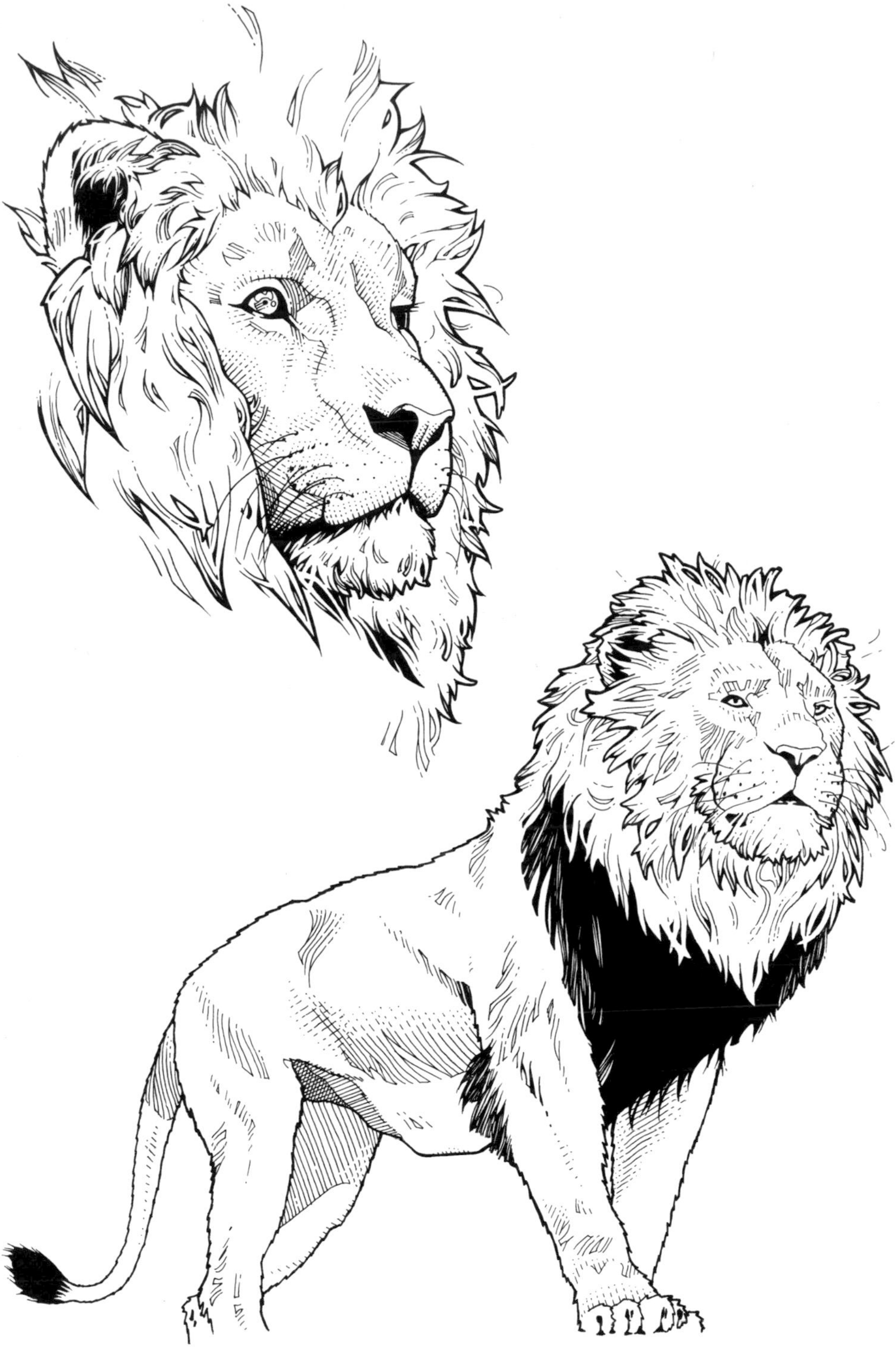

Character sketches of Mufasa.

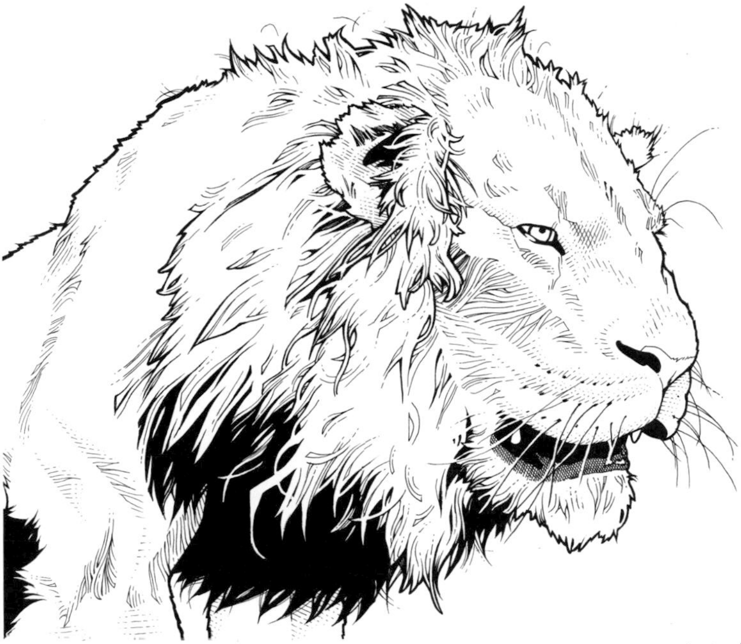

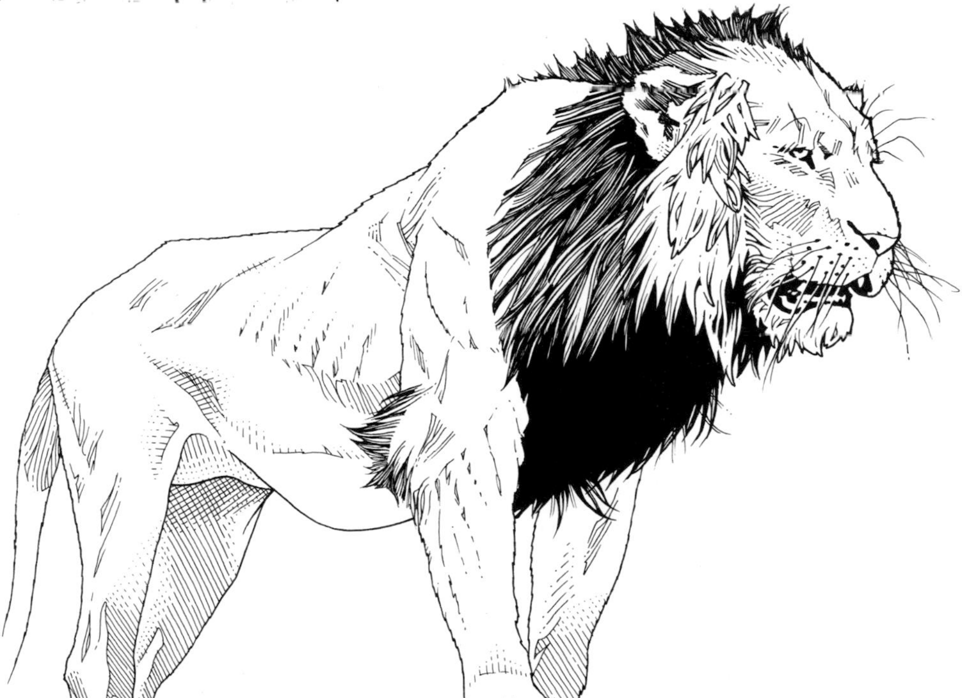

Character sketches of Scar.

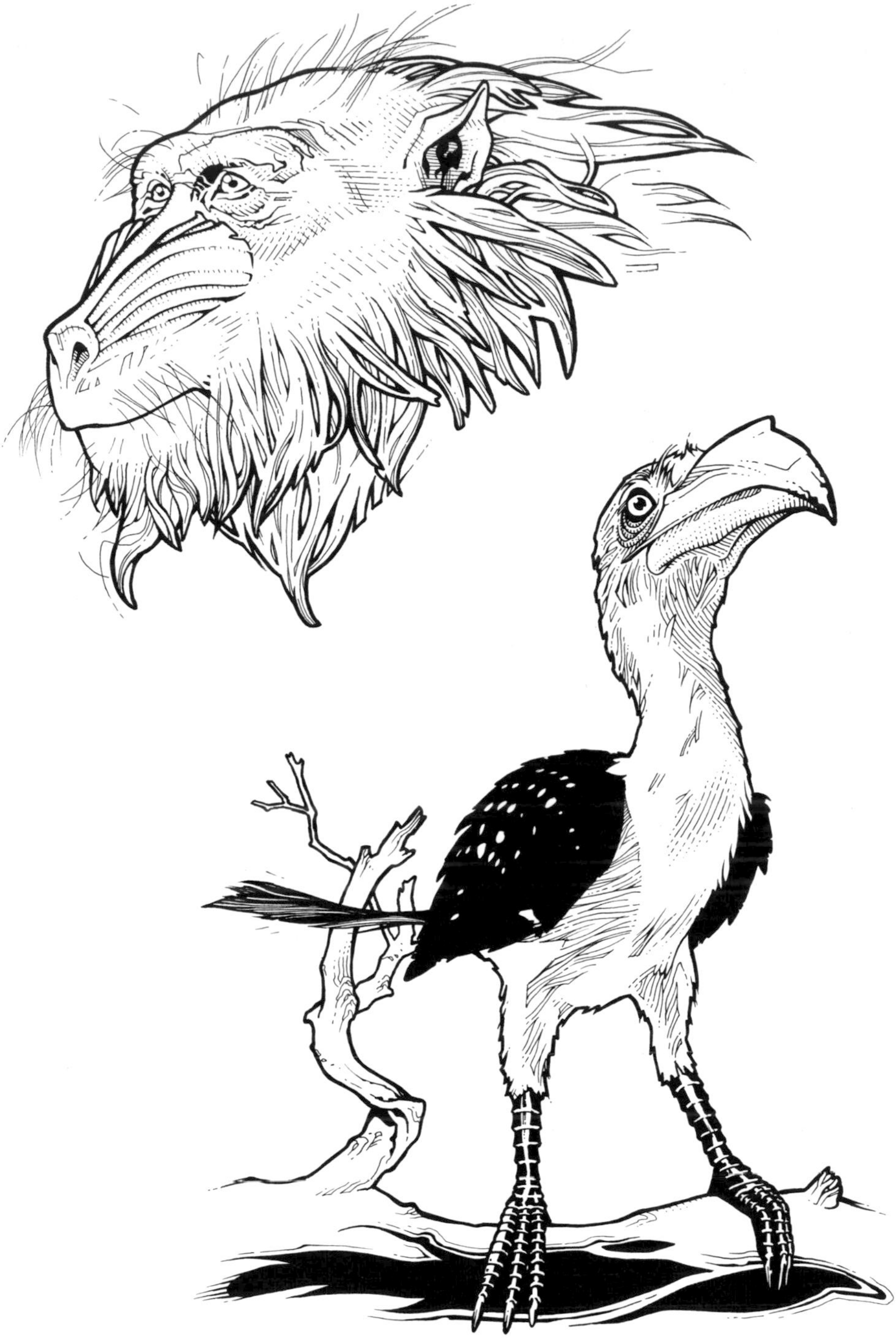

Character sketches of Rafiki and Zazu.

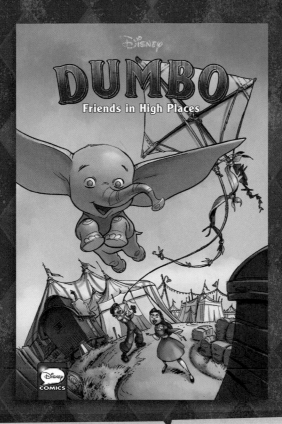

Explore the Medici Brothers Circus from the Disney live-action feature film *Dumbo*, directed by Tim Burton!

Disney Dumbo: Friends in High Places
The beloved story of Dumbo the flying elephant and all his circus friends continues in five interconnected tales. Max Medici's circus is full of curiosity, wonder, and awe—follow Dumbo and friends on a path of discovery—where differences are celebrated and dreams soar.

978-1-50671-268-0 $10.99

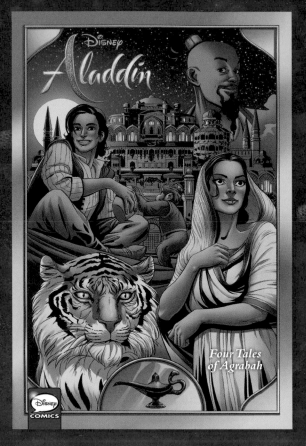

*Take a magic carpet ride through Agrabah
from Disney's all-new film Aladdin!*

Disney Aladdin: Four Tales of Agrabah

Travel through the vibrant city of Agrabah in four tales that
explore the individuality and spirit of *Aladdin*. Follow a day in
the lives of Aladdin, Jasmine, and Genie, and tag along on an
adventure with friends Abu, Raja, and the Magic Carpet!

978-1-50671-267-3 $10.99